Gemma
Bambridge

MADD... WORLD

S.C Dann

To Gemma,

Well done for being our competition
winner! I hope you enjoy
the book! O.O
Ö

Frank

Wilmot

Wallis

Dr Allen

Monty

Lunetta

DAD
(William)

Timothy

Nadine

Eve

Copyright

First published in Great Britain in 2013 with CreateSpace by Samantha Dann

ISBN-13: 978-1492851752
ISBN-10: 1492851752

Thank you…

I would like to thank everyone from the bottom of my heart who supported and encouraged me throughout the writing of this book:

My family. Thank you to my four wonderful children (Avril, Kyle, Niamh and Rhys) for their unwavering love and enthusiasm. As they read each chapter, every smile, laugh and surprised look gave me the confidence to pursue my dream. Their amazing personalities inspired many characters in this book. Thanks to my husband who comforted me when I felt pessimistic and advised me not to give up. I love you all dearly. I am a very lucky woman.

My friends. A special thanks to Janice who read the first manuscript, and Andy who was ignored every evening as Janice giggled through each chapter on their summer holiday. I'd also like to thank Andy for his mischievous personality – many of the characters in Madder's World wouldn't be the same without his friendship. A massive thank you to Caroline who read an updated manuscript and filled me with a boost of much needed confidence. Thanks to Sue and her lovely family, especially her late father (Frank) whose smile and cheeky personality inspired the character named after him in this book. A deep thank you to Betsy for her constant support and the delicious prawn jacket-potatoes. Thanks to Laura who jumps at the chance to join in child-like activities, so I don't look too ridiculous participating on my own – I shall never forget the day at Bewilderwood.

My proofreader. A massive thank you to Andrew Smith who scrutinised every page of Madder's World for grammatical errors. His encouragement and enthusiasm for the story made me more determined than ever to succeed. Seeing the word 'fantastic' written at the end of my completed manuscript will always make me smile.

The illustrator. Thanks to my daughter who has brought the magical images of each precious character locked in my imagination to life. It is a privilege to work with her. I am forever grateful.

My Nan. She died too young but will always live in the happy memory I have of us in our favourite park, speaking to "her" talking mynah bird.

You, the reader. Thank you for buying and taking the time to read this book. I really hope you enjoy it. If you do, please, tell all your friends.

For my husband, my children, Mum and Dad, and my dearest departed Nan – the inspiration behind this book.

Imagine a World

Where has Nanny gone?
Why has she died?
She's gone to heaven.
She's a star in the sky.

What's it like in heaven?
What's it like being a star in the sky?
Nobody knows.
You only find out when you die.

I'll think of her in a place sunny and bright.
Somewhere she can go during the day or at night.
I'll picture huge oak trees and a bird that can talk.
A park where I can join her for walks.

Nanny would love my imaginary place.
How I wish I could see the smile on her face.
So I shut my eyes and go there too.
She's not really dead…
It can't be true.

S C Dann

CHAPTER ONE

Wilmot kicked the empty cola can against the brick wall. The hollow sound echoed as it ricocheted off and clanged along the path. Taking a deep breath, he looked down the damp, narrow alleyway towards School Lane.

Several cars flashed by, water spraying like circular sprinklers off their tyres, as they drove through the puddles on the busy road outside his school. Gilmore Secondary was visible through its perimeter wire fence: the sporadic shrubs had shed their autumn leaves almost overnight.

Wilmot stared at the ugly two-story flat-roofed building – with its red-brick façade and large rectangular windows, defaced by dotted traces of ripped tape from past artwork displays and posters – as he breathed out short, laboured puffs of warm air. In order to get there, he'd have to cross the road – the same road his best friend, Timothy Sparks, died on only two weeks ago.

A nauseous swirl rose from his stomach to his head, leaving him feeling giddy. He swallowed to remove the lump in his throat. Wilmot couldn't go to school today; he wasn't ready to face the dreaded question: did you see it happen?

Yes, he saw the car hit Timothy. Instead of walking with him, like usual, Wilmot had got up late and was lagging behind. He'd seen the whole nightmare unfold like a slow motion scene in a movie as he'd watched from a distance. Wilmot had observed the commotion – the crowd gathered near the motionless body sprawled on the ground – and the arrival of the ambulance. It was only when he'd pushed his way through the crowd of onlookers that he'd felt the devastating punch of grief deep within his chest – it was Timothy, his closest friend since he'd started secondary school over two years ago.

Fixing his gaze on the opposite end of the alleyway, Wilmot exhaled as if the intense grief would disperse into the air, freeing his constricted lungs from the suffocation he felt whenever he stood this close to the school. Tucking both freezing clenched fists in his trouser pockets, he stepped on the can and gritted his teeth as the metal crunched and collapsed under his bodyweight. He couldn't cope with school today – just *one* more day off – he'd feel better tomorrow.

Wilmot swung his leg back and booted the can. It skidded along the concrete path until its crumpled body, now void of air, stopped less than half a metre away from the end of alleyway towards School Lane. His eyes welling with tears, he turned and raced home like a released homing pigeon.

Avoiding eye contact with each passing car, Wilmot looked ahead through the spitting rain – Timothy's killer could be hiding behind any one of those windscreens. The city's weekly newspaper had called the accident a 'hit and run' – left for dead, in his opinion. He swiftly wiped away an escaped tear clinging to his bottom lashes before it dripped on to his cheek, revealing his imprisoned emotions, which weighed down every agonizing step he took like a convict's ball and chain. How could someone knock Timothy over and just drive off? *He was my friend – my best mate!*

As if Timothy's death wasn't enough to deal with right now, Mum broke down in a flood of tears at breakfast and told him it's the tenth anniversary of his father's death. Talk about a great start to the day.

Today's definitely the perfect day to skip school.

Wilmot turned the last corner in to York Avenue, lined on both sides with evenly spaced deciduous trees and identical Victorian semi-detached houses with high pitched triangular roofs, and slowed down as he approached his house. With no sign of Mum's car parked outside, he crept across the road, his eyes darting from one neighbours' window to the next to check if he was being watched, pushed the squeaky wrought iron gate open and slid his key into the lock of his flaky red door.

The house was silent.

Wilmot pulled off his coat and slipped out of his shoes, breathing in the smell of last night's overcooked sausages still lingering in the hallway. Taste buds stimulated, he tiptoed over the cold intricately patterned hallway tiles, through to the cosier carpeted living room – passing, without making guilty eye-contact, the photograph of his mother and father on the mantelpiece above the matt black, horseshoe-shaped fireplace – and over the oak floorboards of the dining room that continued through to the compact pine kitchen at the back of the house. He'd decided to make a sandwich while he thought about which of his favourite films he'd watch later – probably one he'd already watched for the tenth time this last two weeks.

Plonking the plate on the circular dining room table, he sat down – with his mother's voice in his head, telling him not to snack between meals – and took a bite from the chunky sandwich.

THUMP! THUMP! THUMP!

Wilmot jumped up, dropping the sandwich, and stepped away from the table. 'Mum?' he said, almost choking on his mouthful.

THUMP! THUMP! THUMP!

Wilmot felt the thumps vibrate like a series of minor earthquake tremors passing through his feet – the sound definitely wasn't coming from the front door.

13

THUMP!

Gulping down the dry crust wedged in his throat, he stared, watery eyed, at the bread vibrating on the thick blue rug under the table. 'What the…?'

THUMP! THUMP!

Absorbed by curiosity, he slid each of the four solid wood chairs from under the oak table before dragging the cumbersome antique, ignoring the bent corner of the square rug that had caught under one of the bowed table legs, across the room.

Wilmot's eyes widened. He leaned forward, sliding his fingers through his mop of dark brown curly hair to keep it from obscuring his vision, to look at what the peeled-back rug had uncovered. He'd had hundreds, if not thousands, of meals in this room without ever knowing there was a wooden door, over half a metre square, hidden beneath.

Wilmot shuffled closer and scrutinized the slatted wood door, checking for gaps that might reveal a clue to what was below. But there were no gaps. He dislodged a piece of bread stuck between his overlapping front teeth with his tongue and swallowed hard.

Should he open it? Do Mum and Nadine know about the door?

THUMP!

Wilmot jumped back, his heart bouncing in his chest like a basketball, as the door's circular metal latch – set in its own recess, level with the door – rattled with another thump from below. Breathing deeply, he pressed a hand against his chest to ease the hammering inside his ribcage. He had to calm down. How could anything dangerous be trapped under the floor in *his* house?

Wilmot squatted beside the door, slid his shaking finger through the tarnished latch and began to lift. There *had* to be a perfectly logical explanation for the noise. Its stiff hinges creaked open. 'Hello. Is anyone there?' he yelled, his face held close to the floor as he peered through the narrow opening. Did he really expect an answer?

THUMP! THUMP! THUMP!

Wilmot dropped the door, almost wrenching his finger off as he pulled it from the latch, and scrambled to his feet. A thin layer of dust had puffed out of the hole and was now hanging in the air – its odd smell reminded him of his father. He sneezed, dispersing the dust with a fine mist of snot.

Pacing up and down, he sniffed several times to alleviate the tickling sensation irritating the inside of his nose. Why did the smell of the dust remind him of his father? Wilmot sneezed again. Should he really open the door when he had no idea *who* or *what* was making the noise? He wiped his nose on his sleeve. It was probably nothing more than a mouse or a rat, but if he opened the door he might release it into the house – Mum would go mental!

Wilmot stared at the clattering square of wood, nibbling his fingernails, as the thumping continued to vibrate the floor under his feet. Mum would want him to investigate; she'd want him to take a little look – wouldn't she?

After a moment of anxious deliberation, Wilmot spat out his chewed nail, dropped to his knees and began fumbling with the latch. If there was the slightest chance that something was trapped beneath the door and in need of his help, he couldn't walk away. He couldn't just leave and ignore the mysterious noise.

Wilmot *had* to open it.

CHAPTER TWO

Wilmot slid his fingers under the door. Knees bent, he pulled upwards, gradually forcing the stiff, rusty hinges apart. It slowly creaked open until the hinges relented and the door flipped back and slammed against the dining room floor. Wilmot fell forward, taking a giant leap over the hole to avoid falling through.

Staggering, he turned to look at the opening. Engulfed by another waft of dust that had puffed out of the dark hole, he blinked rapidly as tiny granular particles stung his eyes like beach sand blowing off a running child directly into his face. He waved his arms to disperse the dust, mixing the cold air rushing up from below with the warmer air in the room. The sudden change in temperature cooled his face and raised the hairs on his arms like the instant effect of chilling mist rushing out of a chest freezer when the lid is opened.

THUMP! THUMP! THUMP!

Eyes watering, he leaned forward and peered down through the thinning dust at the top of a steep set of narrow wooden steps. 'Is…anyone there?'

There was no reply.

'Please, answer me…is anyone there?' He stared into the blackness, crossing his arms over his chest and rubbing his hands down the sides of his body to keep warm, waiting for a response. But there was still no reply.

Wilmot crouched next to the dark hole, clasping his knees to his chest while he decided what to do next. Perhaps he'd go down a few steps – maybe three or four – just to get a closer look.

Forcing his rigid legs into the hole, he placed a trembling foot on the first step and lowered himself to the next. His heart fluttered erratically like the wings of a startled bat. Was he making the right decision? Should he wait for Mum and go down later? Staring up at the safety of the room disappearing from view, he dangled his foot over the fifth step. Did he really need to take a look right now? After all, playing hero wasn't really…

THUMP! THUMP! THUMP!

Wilmot felt the vibration of every thump pass through his hands and feet, pulsating through his nervous system like a series of small waves breaking on the shore. Wilmot changed direction – he'd definitely go down later.

'AAAAAH!' Wilmot screamed as he lost his footing and fell back. His spine bumped from one hard step to the next until he landed on his back, legs sprawled up the bottom steps, disturbing a blanket of sleeping dust that wafted into the air.

Coughing and spluttering, he lay there like a sack of potatoes waiting for the dust to settle until the last specks lingered like stars in the square moon of light high above.

Wilmot arched his back, dust falling from his thick hair, and slid his hand beneath to rub the tender vertebrae. 'What a *total idiot*.' Massaging his lower back, he lifted himself from the floor.

A strange whimper echoed through the cellar.

Wilmot turned sharply, 'Hello…who's making that n – noise?'

No one answered.

The whimper sounded almost…human?

Curling his toes away from the freezing concrete floor, he shuffled towards the sound. 'Who is it – who's down here?' With each step, his eyes adjusted to the minimal light provided by the room above. He stopped and circled on the spot, scanning the room, breathing short, rapid intakes of air. 'I can't find you. Please, tell me where you are. I want to help.' He blinked away the dust falling from his hair into his eyes.

Still, no one answered.

Wilmot continued forward, his outstretched arms tickling the air in front of him, until his fingers bent back, pressing against something hard. Had he got to the end of the room? He squinted into the dim light. In front of him stood a large object. He patted his fingertips over its dusty, rough surface. It was oblong, standing as high as his chest and about twice as wide, with an indent around its middle, about two thirds of the way up – probably some sort of lid. It felt like a…large wooden box.

Forcing his fingers between the two sections of the box, he bent his knees and pulled upwards in order to move the top section, puffing with every strained movement, until he withdrew involuntarily as a sharp splinter of wood pierced one of his fingertips like a hypodermic needle. It was obvious that he'd need more strength than his puny muscles could muster in order to force it open.

Mystified by what could be inside and how to open it, he stared at the impregnable object, sucking his stinging finger.

THUMP! THUMP! THUMP!

Wilmot jumped back, his pulse racing like an Olympic runner, as the strange whimper started again. There had to be someone trapped inside the box! If something or someone was trapped inside, he had to get them out – right? He couldn't just leave – could he? Wilmot turned to look at the narrow steps – they were only a short distance away. How scary could this thing be? He was in the cellar of *his* house. *Get a grip!*

Taking a deep breath, he stretched the neck of his school sweater and moved forward, arms extended, until his clammy hands made contact with the vibrating box. 'How do I open it?' he asked, his throat tightening with every passing second. 'Any communication you can offer me right now would be a great help,' muttered Wilmot, feeling over the box for another possible opening.

Crouching low, Wilmot felt one, then two and finally three small, circular button-like protrusions on the bottom left-hand side of the box. Would pressing one of them open the box, releasing whatever's trapped inside? He hesitated, holding his fingers over all three of them. Did he *really* want to open it? Folding two fingers back into his palm, he closed his eyes, bit his bottom lip and pressed the top button firmly.

A loud creak echoed through the cellar as the top of the wooden box opened and released a sudden flash of blinding light. Wilmot leaped aside and pressed his back against the cellar wall, flakes of chalky plaster crumbling against his splayed palms, listening to the sounds of bubbling liquids and clinking glass.

Unable to see much in the blinding light, he blinked rapidly to adjust his eyes to the rainbow of colours now lighting the room. Before him stood an experimental bench – the box had transformed into a large bench cluttered with vials containing different coloured liquids connected to bubbling test tubes by clear glass tubes that criss-crossed from one end of the bench to the other. There was everything a scientist would ever need – a scientist just like his dead father!

'Wow!'

Wilmot's voice triggered the thumping sound again. His eyes darted around the room, surveying the active bench, but he saw nothing except the bubbling test tubes and vials. He moved closer and spotted a torch on the bench. Wilmot grabbed the torch, tensing his arm muscles to stop the beam from shaking in his sweaty hands, and turned it on.

'Hello,' said a man's voice.

'Ah!' cried Wilmot, dropping the torch. He glanced over both shoulders as he turned, arms whipping the air at waist height, to check the cellar.

'If you are *not* my wife Madeline, my daughter Nadine or my son Wilmot Madder, you must end this message *now*! If you do not, this message will self-destruct and blast you to smithereens!'

Wilmot continued to scan every inch of the room. 'Who – are – you?' he asked. His chest muscles tightened like stretched elastic as the pre-recorded warning message started again. He spotted a ring of light emitting from the torch, which had landed face down on the floor, and bent down to snatch it before shuffling back towards the steps. 'Explode? The cellar's going to *explode*?' he said, hearing the message a second time.

Wilmot stretched and tightened his fingers around the torch clasped in his trembling hand and clambered up the cellar steps. A third of the way up, he froze, noticing a projected image spreading from the torch across the steps in front of him. Redirecting the beam, he shone the talking image on the cellar wall and stared at the holographic image of a man – a man he knew from distant memories and photographs.

'Dad?' Transfixed by the image, he stepped back and jumped the short distance to the cellar floor.

'This message will self-destruct in ten seconds. Ten – nine – eight – seven–'

'No – no – stop counting!' he pleaded, angling the torchlight to improve the image.

His father's image continued to count while staring straight through Wilmot as if he wasn't in the room. 'Six – five–'

'Please don't...'

'Four – three – two–'

'Nooooo!' On hearing the number one, Wilmot fell to his knees with his arms covering his head. Gasping for air in the disturbed dust, he waited. Moments passed, but nothing happened – no explosion – only the sounds of bubbling liquids filled the room.

'If you remained in the cellar, congratulations, you've just passed your first test of courage.'

Wilmot lowered his arms, directing the torch beam back on the cellar wall, and stared in bewilderment at the transparent life-size moving image of his father. Dad had the same disordered mass of thick, dark brown hair – which he had been unfortunate enough to inherit – a shadow where his beard was beginning to show at least a day's new growth, and the familiar deep furrow lines across his forehead on his otherwise smooth and kind-looking face. Although Dad still looked tall and slim, he did appear significantly shorter than the imposing figure he used to gaze up at as a young child. Then, Wilmot noticed the old lab coat his father was wearing. No matter what day of the week or what the weather, he couldn't recall his father ever wearing anything else. It was this stained coat, Wilmot remembered, that'd carried the dusty smell which had reminded him of his father when he'd first opened the cellar door.

Wilmot knew his father was dead, and that he was unable to interact with this emotionless, pre-recorded image, but this was unbelievable after ten years with nothing but a few photos!

'Amazing,' said Wilmot, rising to his feet.

The hologram continued: 'Hopefully I *am* talking to a member of my family, and that your visit to the cellar has coincided with the end of Frank's ten-year hibernation. If this is correct, both of my dear children are now old enough to endure the journey ahead.'

The image started to flicker and fade, making the message increasingly distant and unclear. 'Come on...' said Wilmot, shaking the torch. 'Don't stop now!'

Dad's voice returned for a few seconds before it tailed off again and continued intermittently: '...underneath the bench...a perfect disguise...be careful...don't bounce...' Nothing made any sense.

Wilmot shook the torch again, but it made no difference – Dad's voice came and disappeared again like an interrupted phone connection on a journey through a series of short tunnels.

'Batteries – it needs new batteries,' he muttered. After checking the torch several times, he gave up: the torch had no battery compartment.

'...he will protect you....' Then the sound disappeared altogether.

'Dad! Come back!' he cried at the fading image. 'Good luck,' repeated Wilmot, lip-reading his father's words, '...meet – again – in – Madder's World.'

Dad's image disappeared.

Wilmot switched the torch on and off and shook it vigorously again and again. But nothing made it work. 'What am I supposed to do now?' He groaned in frustration as he slumped to the floor. Could he make sense of what little he'd heard? Madder was his surname – why would his father speak of a world named after their family? And who was Frank?

THUMP! THUMP! THUMP!

Wilmot's eyes were drawn to a small brown suitcase, under the experimental bench, which seemed to have developed a life of its own. With each thump the case lifted and fell back against the concrete floor, scraping its already worn leather.

Wilmot scrambled to his feet and moved closer. Each approaching footstep seemed to soothe the case: its angry thump reduced to a calm rocking motion, until it finally stopped altogether.

Wilmot stood over the motionless suitcase. 'At last,' he said, '*that's* where the noise is coming from.'

CHAPTER THREE

Wilmot reached forward, slid the case towards him, and held his thumbs against the two rusty clasps – a sideways movement of both hands was all that stood between him and what lurked inside. Taking a deep breath, he applied pressure. The case sprang open and flipped back, disturbing the sleeping dust as it hit the cellar floor.

Wilmot froze. His eyes followed something darting through the suspended dust. Did it just escape from the case?

'Who's there?' He coughed, ingesting even more throat drying dust.

Nothing. Had he imagined it?

After scanning the room several times, Wilmot gave up and focused back on the case, which had been filled to the brim with a colourful variety of odd socks, and began to rummage through. There had to be more than a pile of socks inside – socks don't whimper, and they certainly don't make thumping noises without feet in them.

When he'd checked and thrown almost every sock to one side, Wilmot noticed a tiny box resting at the bottom of the case. He picked the box up and carefully pulled open its magnetically held mirrored lid, disturbing several marble-like balls rolling around the limited space within its shiny, black interior.

'AAAAAH!' Wilmot squealed like a mouse caught in a trap. An intense pain shot through his buttocks as if he'd fell on a spiny cactus, making him drop the box, scattering the marbles all over the cellar floor. Frantically waving his hands near his bum, he began turning in circles. 'OWW!' Teeth clenched, he arched his back and looked over his shoulder to see what was hanging from his bottom. 'AAAAAH!' He winced, wiggling his rear in the hope it'd drop off, but the hold on his tender flesh was too strong. The pain intensified, shooting through his buttocks like a hundred shrapnel wounds piercing one delicate area of skin. He had to get it off – *now*! Clenching his fist, he swung his arm back and punched the small round creature.

Despite the heavy blow, it hung on refusing to let go. '*Please – get off me!*'

As if Wilmot had just discovered the correct command, the creature released its grip and fell with a plop to the floor. Breathing through his nostrils like a rhinoceros ready to charge, Wilmot turned to glare at the offending bum-biter.

Sitting in a little dust pit was the strangest thing Wilmot had seen in his entire life. About the size of a small orange (although pale yellow in colour) it had no defined body, with two thin legs and arms that stuck out on either side of its bulbous head. The creature grinned mischievously back at him. Its huge square teeth, set perfectly straight on its upper and lower jaw, were completely disproportionate to the rest of its features.

'What the…what are you? And why did you bite me?' he asked, placing two hands over his buttocks in case the creature decided to bite him again. 'I'm insane…what – am – I – talking to?'

'Me Frank.' It spoke quickly in a high-pitched voice.

'Ah!' cried Wilmot, stepping back. 'You can *actually* speak?'

'Frank sorry. Been in case for ten years – make Frank bit nutty. Frank not bite Wilmot again.' His all-teeth grin spread across the entire width of his face.

'What, *exactly*, are you? And how do you know my name?'

'I'm a mucker – means friend. William Madder made Frank. He told me your name.'

'My *father* made you?' Frank got up and waddled towards him. Wilmot shuffled back. 'Don't come any closer!' Tripping over his own feet, he fell on his sore bottom. Without hesitation, Frank jumped straight on to Wilmot's legs and began to work his way up. 'Get off me!' protested Wilmot, jiggling his legs to shake him off. Undeterred, Frank positioned his weightless body on Wilmot's lap and gripped his trousers with both tiny hands. 'Get off!' he continued, still shaking both legs. Frank bounced in his lap like an anchored buoy battling the waves until Wilmot finally gave up.

For a few awkward moments, they sat gawking at one another.

Wilmot eventually broke the silence and asked, 'Are you going to bite me again?'

Frank shook his head.

Silence.

'Did I hear you correctly – did you say that my father made you?' Frank nodded.

Silence.

'So you expect me to believe you've been stuck down here on your own...for ten years?'

'Frank's been hibernating.'

'Hibernating,' repeated Wilmot, 'for *ten years?* Let me get this right, a speaking...blob has been hibernating in a secret cellar in my house for ten whole years, wearing – what is that you're wearing on your head?' he asked, leaning forward to take a closer look. 'A sock? Why are you wearing a stripy orange and white sock on your head?'

'Frank like sock,' he answered, grinning. 'And I'm not a blob – I'm a mucker!'

'And what, exactly, are you made of?' Wilmot gave him a poke before retracting his finger as if he'd just touched something very hot. 'Urgh, you're all soft and…' He grimaced, unable to finish his sentence.

'Frank made of synthetic skin. Frank shows you.' He jumped off Wilmot's lap, scurried over to the experimental bench and pressed the second in the series of buttons that Wilmot had found earlier. A row of suspended vials burst into life as the liquid inside began to bubble furiously. 'Wilmot needs new skin if going to Madder's World.'

'New skin? Madder's World? What are you talking about *now*?'

Frank climbed up the bench, grabbed a long pair of hanging tweezers and placed them into a bubbling vial containing red liquid.

'What are you doing?' asked Wilmot.

Hovering precariously over the vial, Frank teased the tweezers in and out as if he were trying to catch something.

Wilmot moved closer. 'What are all these tiny things floating inside the liquid?' he asked, trying to focus on one swirling at the bottom of the vial.

'Got one!' Without warning, Frank pulled the tweezers from the vial.

As soon as the thing on the end of the tweezers came in contact with the air, it grew rapidly. Before Wilmot had time to move, the thing expanded and punched him in the face. Launched across the room, he landed, on his painful bottom, and lifted his dizzy head to find Frank balancing something that resembled an enormous leg on the end of the tweezers.

Frank jumped off the bench and waddled towards him with the humungous leg swaying like an over-inflated balloon above his head.

'*That's* going nowhere near me!' exclaimed Wilmot, blinking to regain focus.

'Wilmot put on new leg.'

'No way! I'd look like a circus freak with a leg as big as that! Is it really that massive?' He squinted, feeling quite sure his eyes were playing tricks on him after his sudden 'out of body' experience.

'Leg not stay big when on Wilmot.'

Frank dropped the leg, leaving it to bounce once before it knocked into the bottoms of Wilmot's dusty socks, and hurried back to the bench.

'What's going on? I *am* going mad,' mumbled Wilmot, retracting his feet and clutching his knees to his chest. 'Strange creatures, synthetic skin and now I'm expected to get *new* legs.' He slid his outstretched fingers through his hair before interlocking them at the back of his neck.

'All make sense soon,' said Frank, dragging a spray bottle back. 'Wilmot must do what Frank say.' Before Wilmot was able to utter another word, Frank gripped the bottom of one of his trouser legs with his teeth and pulled. ' –'ilmot – 'ousers – off!'

'Get off me!' he protested, grasping for the loose trouser waistband sliding swiftly over his slim belly. 'I'm not taking my trousers off!' Moments later, his trousers were yanked down his legs, over his knees and left to bunch at his ankles. 'What are you *doing*?' Wilmot clumsily shuffled back before attempting to stand, but collapsed to the floor as Frank continued to tug his trousers like a wilful puppy, pulling them over his feet and tossing them triumphantly to one side – closely followed by his socks – before he'd had the chance to regain his balance.

Within seconds, Frank picked up the huge leg and pulled it over one of Wilmot's legs like a giant sock. Wilmot kicked out to try to shake the leg off. But Frank was already in position with the spray gun in both hands. He pushed on the pump action trigger – spraying every inch of his leg until it was completely covered in thick, clear liquid – as if he was a cowboy firing bullets from a pistol in a gunfight.

The synthetic skin shrank tight against Wilmot's skin. 'What are you doing to me?' he protested. A strange tickling sensation tingled up and down his leg. 'Make it stop!' Pinching his leg, Wilmot pulled at the synthetic skin as it continued to tighten over his actual skin like an over-stretched latex glove. 'It tickles! Please, make it stop!' Wilmot flopped to the concrete floor, his limbs flailing, writhing around in an uncontrollable fit of laughter.

Seemingly oblivious to Wilmot's distress, Frank started licking the dusty floor. 'Yummy.'

After about thirty seconds, the tickling sensation finally stopped.

Breathless from his ordeal, Wilmot sat up and looked down at his leg. 'Did it...fall off?'

'Not fallen off. Fusion Spray worked. Wilmot has new leg skin,' informed Frank, licking his lips.

Wilmot stood up. 'My new leg doesn't look any different to my other one.' He pressed his two legs together to compare them. 'The synthetic skin must have combined with my own skin: it's the same colour, it has the same fine hairs – everything's the same. What's the point in that?' Wilmot grimaced at Frank still licking the floor. 'What are you doing?'

'Frank hungry. Frank love Fusion Spray,' he replied, followed by a grin that revealed his dust-covered teeth.

'Yuk! You ate the spray off the floor.' He picked Frank up and dangled him in mid air. 'You must go to the toilet if you eat.' He tilted his head to look at

Frank's underside. 'You're nothing but a fat head with arms and legs. No bum…not a hole in sight.'

'Wilmot need new skin on other leg, then arms and head before go to Madder's World.' Frank wriggled free, plopped to the floor and toddled off towards the bench.

'I don't understand – why do *I* need to go to this place? Where is Madder's World, and why do I need new skin to go there?'

'Wilmot knows when he get there.'

'Great! Wilmot knows when he get there,' he repeated, mimicking Frank's high-pitched voice. 'I might not want to go – have you thought about that?' Cursing Frank in an incoherent mutter, Wilmot followed him to the experimental bench. 'And what are all these things floating inside the other vials?' he asked, looking at the different coloured liquids. 'More lovely surprises for me – a new *brain* perhaps?' he asked, sarcastically. 'I need a new brain for letting *you* out of that case!'

Far too busy fishing with the tweezers in the red vial, Frank ignored Wilmot. Within seconds, he'd pulled out another leg that expanded as quickly as the last.

'No way! Not again!' exclaimed Wilmot, backing off.

After much protest, Frank managed to pull on Wilmot's other leg skin and spray it. Another thirty seconds of uncontrollable laughter and agonising discomfort followed before both of Wilmot's legs were finally covered in synthetic skin.

'If you think you're coming anywhere near me again,' said Wilmot, putting his socks and trousers back on, 'then you're…' Wilmot stood up. Zipping his trousers, he looked around. 'Frank! Where are you? Frank, hiding from me isn't funny!' he exclaimed, remaining vigilant in a knees bent posture in case Frank sprang out of nowhere with more synthetic skin. His foot knocked against a small ball sat on the floor next to him. 'Frank?' he said, noticing a small piece of the sock Frank had been wearing poking out of the ball.

Pop! Pop! Pop! Pop!

With each pop, one of Frank's limbs appeared – including the hand still holding the sock – closely followed by his eyes, nose and mouth.

'How did you do th–?'

Suck! Suck! Suck! Suck!

Before Wilmot had finished his sentence, Frank took a deep breath, closed his eyes and mouth and sucked all of his limbs into his body. Frank had transformed back into a ball!

'Wow! I'll be able to take you anywhere with a disguise like that! Do you bounce too?' Muffled protests came from within the ball. 'You *do* bounce. Amazing!' he said, watching the ball hit the floor and bounce back up in front of him.

Frank gradually gained height and hit the cellar ceiling. He ricocheted off, crashing into the end of the experimental bench. Everything wobbled, then, like collapsing dominoes, the contents on the bench began to topple. The glass vials and test tubes fell, one after the other, smashing against the floor like a series of small explosions, spurting little fountains of broken glass and liquid into the air.

'Frank! Stop!' Running from one end of the cellar to the other, Wilmot tried to catch Frank as he careered from the floor to the ceiling and back into the bench. 'Frank! Stop bouncing!'

Experimental equipment continued to fall and shatter, littering the cellar floor with puddles of coloured liquid and glass, until almost everything was destroyed. With no hope of catching him, Wilmot gave up and stood, jaw gaping, watching the final few vials tumble and smash.

Silence fell upon the cellar.

Frank finally stopped bouncing, leaving every bubbling vial and every test tube on the bench broken. Coloured liquid dripped from the bench to the floor to form a luminous mass of merging colours at Wilmot's feet.

'Frank! Where are you?' Hobbling through the debris, he tried to avoid the slivers of sharp, wet glass jabbing at his feet. 'Are you hurt? Frank! Speak to me! Don't die – please, don't die.'

Pop! Pop! Pop! Pop!

Wilmot felt something tugging his trousers. 'Frank, are you okay?' He picked Frank up and checked him over. 'I can't believe it – there's not a single scratch on you,' he said, turning him one way and then the other. 'How–?'

'Frank indestructible!'

'*You* might be indestructible, but look at this place – total annihilation,' said Wilmot, looking all around him. 'How am I going to clear this lot up before Mum and Nadine come home? I don't even know if *they* know about the cellar.'

SLAM!

'Oh no, that's the front door,' whispered Wilmot, stuffing Frank, who instantly transformed back into a ball, into his trouser pocket. 'No one can see the cellar now – not like this.'

Total disaster! He had to get out – fast!

Wilmot ran to the cellar steps.

CHAPTER FOUR

Wilmot darted up the cellar steps, hauled himself through the hatch and shut the cellar door behind him.

'Wilmot, is that you?'

'Yes, Mum!' he answered, panting. He grasped the rug and dragged it back over the cellar door.

'I'm just nipping upstairs to the toilet!'

Phew! Just a few more moments and everything would be back to normal. He pulled the table over the rug, placing each leg into the deep, dusty indentations it had made previously. With seconds to spare, he pushed the last of the chairs under the table as Mum's footsteps came back down the stairs.

'You're home quick today,' she said, her petite frame leaning against the doorframe as Wilmot rushed back into the living room to greet her. 'I'm shattered. I had to make two massive funeral bouquets this morning – ridiculous – I'm going to have to find another florist that appreciates the time it takes to achieve perfection.' She untied her ponytail, forced her hands through her dark wiry hair and shook it, releasing the intoxicating scent of flowers. 'Wilmot, are your feet *bleeding*?'

Wilmot looked down at the beige carpet, his eyes flitting from one small patch of blood to the next. 'I – I trod on some broken gla…' How was he going to get out of this? Whether she knew about the secret cellar or not, Frank had destroyed it now, and she'd be devastated if she found out. 'It's nothing, Mum, my feet are fine.' Why were there patches of blood on the floor when he couldn't feel any pain?

'Did you drop a drinking glass? Have you picked up all the broken pieces?' she asked, following a trail of dotted blood to the dining room table.

'Err, yes, I put them in the outside bin.' Wilmot lifted each foot and removed his dusty black socks. He'd felt the broken glass under his feet but hadn't realised his feet were actually bleeding.

'Let me see your feet.'

'No, I'm all right.'

'Sit down and I'll bring you a nice warm bowl of salt water to bathe them.'

He hobbled to the sofa on his heels, preparing himself for his mother's next unanswerable question, and sat down.

'It looks like you've picked up all the glass. You didn't spill a drop of drink anywhere either!'

'I'd finished the drink.' His neck sank into his shoulders as he lied along with his mother's assumption. *Please – please stop looking under the table.*

'It's unusual to have you home first – Nadine's usually back before you!'

Wilmot glanced at the clock on the mantelpiece. He'd been in the cellar longer than he'd thought. Very different from the last two weeks he'd spent either hanging around the local graveyard or at home watching movie after movie – something she was, thankfully, still unaware of.

'Stick your feet in there,' she insisted, placing a bowl at his feet. Some of the water slopped over the sides on to the carpet.

'Hi, Mum!' The door slammed shut and Nadine's tall stick-like body came charging into the living room. Her long, straight brown hair fell flat against her cheeks as she stopped suddenly and looked at Wilmot who was instantly reminded of how much she resembled their father. 'How did *you* get home so quickly? You're like some *invisible being* – I never see you at school, and then you seem to appear out of nowhere!'

'Shut up,' snapped Wilmot, looking over his shoulder to check whether or not his mother had heard Nadine on her way out of the room.

'You shut up!' she retorted, heading to the kitchen. 'Hi, Mum.'

'Now that you're both home, I've got something important to ask you,' said Mum, making her way back to the living room with Nadine following close behind. 'I've some exciting news. The science convention, which I'm going to tomorrow, have just informed me that they are to hold a tribute speech in memory of your father. It's to commemorate the tenth anniversary of his death. I'd love you both to come with me?'

Wilmot sighed inwardly. 'I'll come.' Normally he'd be more than willing, but what he really needed right now was time alone to go back in the cellar and sort things out.

'They'll be all of Dad's old friends there.'

'What fun,' muttered Nadine. 'I'll see how I feel in the morning.'

'You'll miss a day's school,' added Mum.

'Boring conference or boring school – what an exciting choice,' muttered Nadine.

Pop! Pop!

Wilmot gripped his trouser pocket, squashing Frank, in order to hinder his transformation.

'You disgusting excuse for a brother!'

'What? It wasn't me!' protested Wilmot, without thinking.

'Oh, right – who was it then? I can't see anyone else on the *smelly* side of the room.'

Glaring at Nadine, he remained quiet – he'd have to take the blame for a bad case of wind this time.

'How are your feet?' Mum bent down and lifted his foot from the bowl of water. 'Mmm...no cuts,' she said, frowning. 'That's odd.'

Warm water trickled up his leg. 'Don't fuss, Mum, I'm fine,' he said, pulling his foot away. He stepped out of the bowl and stood on the towel his mother had just placed on the floor, wiping his feet vigorously back and forth.

'What's wrong with my, *baby* brother?' teased Nadine.

'Oh, shut up!' Nudging past Nadine, standing a head taller than him, he looked at the spots of dried blood on the carpet – why had his feet healed already? Keeping a firm grip on his pocket, he left the room before he suffocated Frank.

As soon as he reached his bedroom, he closed the door and leaned against it to make sure no one else could enter without a fight. 'If I let go, you need to keep quiet,' whispered Wilmot, loosening his grip on his trouser pocket.

Pop! Pop!

With his hand placed securely over Frank's big mouth, Wilmot pulled him from his pocket. A wet, sticky tongue circled the palm of Wilmot's hand. 'Urgh, that's *gross*.' He grimaced, tossing Frank into his other hand, before wiping the spit down his trousers.

Frank's mischievous all-teeth grin spread across his face. 'Frank wants meet Madeline and Nadine.'

'How do you know their names?'

'Wilmot dad told me when he told me Wilmot's name.'

'Shh! Keep your voice down. So, Dad made you before he died?' Frank nodded. 'Out of synthetic skin that can heal quicker than I can think?' Frank nodded again. 'And now you're going to help me get to a place called Madder's World?'

The door clicked open and thumped against his shoulder, jolting him sideways. Digging his heals into the carpet, he pushed against the door to force it shut.

'Talking to yourself is the first sign of madness you know!' teased Nadine. 'Even if you are living in an *imaginary* world!' She laughed.

'Get lost, Nadine!' he yelled, stuffing Frank back into his pocket.

'Don't worry – *I* won't tell anyone!'

Wilmot pushed harder, wedging his outstretched legs between the door and his wardrobe, as the door bumped repeatedly against his body. The door handle rubbed Wilmot's shoulder, chafing his skin, as Nadine wiggled it up and down in frustration. After one last determined push, she released the door handle and headed back downstairs. 'I don't want to go in your stinky bedroom anyway!' she exclaimed.

Not an hour had passed since he'd been out of the cellar and Nadine had already heard too much. In future he'd have to be more careful and speak to Frank when they were alone – it was far too risky with her around.

To ensure Frank remained hidden in his bedroom, he made up a story about a fierce bearded man who stole bouncing balls and never gave them back. Only when he saw the whites of Frank's round eyes bulging back at him, and he was sure he'd scared him enough, did he tuck him securely under his pillow and sneak out of his room to go downstairs to eat his dinner.

Two hours of fake yawning, on the pretence he'd had a stressful day at school, and Wilmot finally headed back upstairs for an early night. When he returned to his room, he was relieved to find Frank quietly sleeping, without a single sign of any bounce damage to his room, in exactly the same spot he'd left him.

Wilmot got into his pyjamas and curled up under his duvet. Staring at the shadows from a tree outside his window flickering across his prized car posters, stuck randomly over his otherwise plain magnolia bedroom walls, he tried to piece the day's events together. Nothing made any sense. He'd have to wait and talk to Frank when they were alone tomorrow. Frank was the only link between him and his father's failed message. He rolled over and shut his eyes.

Drifting in and out of sleep, periodically glimpsing at the time on his alarm clock, he prayed the night would pass quickly.

Wilmot was quite sure everything would be clearer after a good sleep.

CHAPTER FIVE

Wilmot checked the luminous hands on his bedside clock. It was midnight. Restless, he sat up and rubbed his tingling legs.

'Frank,' he whispered, lifting his pillow.

'Any sign of Bearded Man?' asked a very sleepy-eyed Frank. 'Will not come and take Frank away?' He yawned.

'Err…no…he's not here. What's wrong with my legs? My legs feel…strange.'

'It's time!' said Frank. His eyes pinged open with sudden alertness. He stretched the end of his stripy sock and placed it snugly on his head.

'Time? Time for what?'

Frank gripped the duvet with his teeth and pulled it to the floor.

Wilmot stood up and shook his legs to ease the increasing irritation. 'What's happening?' he asked, rubbing his hands up and down his thighs.

'Wilmot needs walk to make better.' Frank grabbed Wilmot's left foot and pulled him towards the bedroom door.

'What are you doing? It's midnight,' he protested, hopping forward on one leg.

'Best time to go to Madder's World – nobody see us in dark.' Frank kept on pulling.

'But how do we get there?'

'Where does Wilmot normally go to be with father?' Frank sprang into the air, landed on the door handle and pushed it down. He let go and fell to the floor. The door swung open.

'Frank, I can't go to my father's grave *now*,' he whispered, tersely. Frank scurried along the landing to the top of the stairs and gestured at Wilmot to follow. 'Wait there,' he added through gritted teeth as Frank disappeared from view.

Wilmot's mind filled with the vivid image of his father's grave. His imagination seemed more enhanced than usual. An overwhelming urge came over him – he had to leave the house – he had to get to the church and to his father's grave. His legs were as anxious as his mind to leave, which was ludicrous – why would he need to go *there* now?

Wilmot stepped on to the landing and stared at his mother's bedroom door. Amazed she hadn't woken already, he crept past her door and Nadine's, avoiding each known creaky floorboard, until he reached the top of the stairs in time to see Frank push the key in the front door lock. Gripping the key with his teeth, Frank turned it, grinding metal to metal, as he forced it unsuccessfully one way and then the other.

Should he really follow Frank at such a ridiculous hour? He was still dressed in his blue checked pyjamas. Wilmot looked back at his mother's bedroom door and almost called out for her help when he heard the front door click open. Wide-eyed, he watched Frank run through the open door. Frank's gone? Left the house without caring whether he'd follow him or not! A shot of adrenaline flooded his pounding heart like rainwater seeping into the cracks of a dry riverbed. Decision made – he had to follow him now.

Wilmot sat at the top of the banister, slid down and jumped off before hitting the newel at the bottom. He put on his shoes, grabbed his coat and shut the door quietly behind him.

A layer of frost had already coated Mum's car parked outside. Jogging at a steady pace, breathing out puffs of hot air, he unravelled the tucked-in arms of his coat before putting it on. His eyes remained fixed on Frank running ahead as he continued under the hazy glow of each streetlamp dotting the frosty pavement in front of him. The full moon remained constant, guiding his way like a huge spotlight.

When he finally caught up with Frank, the irritation in his legs had eased. 'These new legs are awesome,' said Wilmot. 'I'm running faster than I've ever run before.'

'Now Wilmot can copy Frank.'

Frank sped off again. His little legs were a blur. Instead of avoiding the next lamppost, he swung round it and leaped on to the nearest parked car. He bounced from one bonnet to the next before jumping off and landing on a garden wall. At the end of the wall, he leaped on to a conveniently placed wheelie bin before tumbling back to the ground.

Wilmot had seen something like this on television. A man had gone unaided and on foot through a busy city, using every obstacle in his path to speed up his journey, faster than another man who was trying to beat him in a car. The man on foot (free running) had won!

Instead of running past the next post box, Wilmot copied Frank: a quick leapfrog and he was over it. Then, he jumped up and landed on a nearby car. Its metal bonnet buckled on impact. He hesitated on all fours, looking up at the adjacent house, hoping no one had heard. Holding his breath, he waited…not a single curtain twitched. He cartwheeled to the ground – too excited to wait any longer. Wilmot was free running too!

After several challenging obstacles, and in half the time it normally took to reach the church, Wilmot spotted the tall spire towering above the last set of terraced houses. He turned the final corner, skidded on an icy puddle and stopped abruptly behind Frank facing the building that had come to symbolise his father's death.

The moon had arrived before him, hanging above the picturesque church, its light enhancing the sparkling frost on the gravestones and grass below like a scattering of precious stones. Its tall steeple stood to the left, while the rest of the building extended to the right, adorned with beautiful stained glass windows that glimmered in the moonlight. It shadowed the crematorium beyond where loved-ones were more commonly laid to rest. This was a special place. It was the place Wilmot came to be alone, where he talked to his dead father – something he had done almost every day since Timothy's death.

An icy breeze whisked up the damp leaves at Wilmot's feet, disturbing his thoughts. He shuddered as a cold shiver passed down the entire length of his spine like a slithering snake seeking warmth. 'Graveyards are much scarier at night,' he whispered, bending down to pick Frank up. Wilmot wiggled the latch on the small, wooden churchyard gate until it clicked open. Its frosty surface melted against his warm fingers. 'Are you sure this is a good idea?' He glanced back. 'Maybe we should go back home?'

Frank shook his head. 'Wilmot must come with Frank.'

Wilmot walked forward and let go of the gate. It sprang shut, hitting the backs of his legs, its squeaky hinges disturbing the eerie silence. 'This is *way* too scary. I really think we should go home.'

'Frank not scared.'

'That's because…well, you're not even *human.*' Frank looked quite offended. 'Okay – I'm sorry – I'll come with you. But the first sign of a weirdo in there and I'm off home, whether you come with me or not.'

Wilmot shuffled across the path, turning left in the direction of his father's grave. The icy gravel crunched as it separated beneath his feet. Passing under a row of overhanging trees, eyes shifting from one gnarled bare branch to the next, he continued forward until he reached the end of the path where he stepped on to some overgrown, frost-covered grass growing between two large gravestones. A brittle twig snapped underfoot. He turned sharply, his heart pounding in his chest like the beat of a bass drum. Unable to see anyone, he exhaled and moved on.

In need of a distraction, he began reading some of the names on the gravestones. He mumbled through the names he couldn't pronounce and bypassed those out of the moonlight.

Some gravestones were small and simple while others were large and ornate. Several had sunk into the ground, often leaning to one side, the majority of which were covered in lichen and far too worn to be legible. A few were tended with fresh flowers, wilted by the frost, but most were overgrown and forgotten.

Wilmot stumbled sideways in the pitted earth, snagging his coat on an overhanging branch. 'Frank!' Another branch, separated at its end into several thin branches, each one with nodules resembling swollen joints, reached out like the long fingers of an aged hand, snagging his sleeve. 'Fraaaaank heeeeelp meeeee!' He jerked his arm repeatedly to free the entangled fabric. Twisting his body in a contorted spin, he pulled his arms from his sleeves and ran to a safe distance before turning to look at his coat dangling from the tree. Frank crawled out of the sleeve, unhooked the coat and fell with it to the ground.

Wilmot took a deep breath. 'It's *only* a tree. Talk about being in need of a reality check. I'm a complete wreck. I need to chill out.' He retrieved his coat, brushed it down and put it back on.

Frank sniggered. 'Wilmot very funny.'

'This whole panic-I-think-I'm-going-to-die thing seems to be amusing you! Well, it's not funny! This was your *stupid* idea, and I'm *not* laughing!'

'But Wilmot *is* funny.'

'Hilarious – I'm totally rib-achingly hilarious,' he added, sarcastically. He sighed deeply. 'Now be quiet, so I can get my bearings and locate my father's grave – everything looks really different at night.'

Wide-eyed, Wilmot surveyed the graveyard – it had definitely been a mistake to watch *Sleepy Hollow* (one of his mother's horror films) yesterday. In fact, everything around him seemed to spark off something he'd watched in a film recently. Being in a graveyard with an overactive imagination was a seriously bad combination.

'There it is.' He picked Frank up and headed towards his father's grave.

Withered in the cold, splayed like spider legs, were the flowers Wilmot had left only two days ago in front of his father's simple Gothic arch gravestone. He stepped on to his father's grave and knelt down to rearrange the dying stems. An owl hooted in the creaking branches of a large oak tree above him.

'What do we do now?' asked Wilmot, his teeth chattering now that he was no longer running to keep warm.

'How deep Wilmot's father buried?' asked Frank.

'How *deep*? I've no time for stupid games. Don't you realise how *creepy* all this is?'

'How deep?' Frank grinned back at him.

'You're *really* annoying me now.'

'How deep?'

'How should I know?' Wilmot turned on the spot – his enhanced imagination still seemed to be playing tricks on him: every tree trunk and branch seemed to show a twisted, deathly resemblance to the human form. 'This isn't funny, Frank.'

Frank waited for an answer.

'I don't know. He's probably six feet under!' The earth shifted beneath his feet. Wilmot's shoes sank into the soil. 'I'm stuck! I can't move!'

'*Repeat the thoughts in your head, until you think you might be dead.*' Frank began to chant a rhyme.

'What's happening? Frank! Stop!' Wilmot held out his arms to try to steady himself as the earth beneath his feet continued to bulge and churn as if several giant earthworms had gathered to gorge on the soil's nutrients.

'*Look down to the ground. Travel fast without much sound.*' Frank continued with the rhyme. '*Most of you will be there. Think hard now, Wilmot, don't despair.*'

Frank repeated the rhyme over and over again.

'What does all that mean?' cried Wilmot, listening to each word while struggling to remain upright in the sinking earth. He unwittingly repeated the words in his head as the rhyme instructed. 'Frank, *shut up*! You're not helping!' Wilmot stuffed him in his pocket.

Seconds later, the ground collapsed beneath his feet. He reached up and seized a handful of overhanging grass. Lumps of crumbling earth fell on to his face, spotting his blinking eyes with dirt, as he dangled into the open grave ready to swallow him like the mouth of a ravenous predator.

'Frank! Help me!' His body jolted downwards as the roots holding the clump of grass began to give way. Another small jerk and the grass ripped free.

'AAAAAH!' Wilmot screamed as he plunged into the darkness.

CHAPTER SIX

Wilmot plummeted deeper and deeper. He reached out, grabbing at the muddy walls to stop his decent, but the soft, damp clumps just crumbled in his hands and fell to the depths below.

Unable to see anything in the blackness, he shut his eyes telling himself it wasn't happening – he wasn't falling – this *couldn't* be happening to him! Using his enhanced imagination, he began to pretend he was travelling more comfortably. Instead of falling into his father's grave, Wilmot imagined he was travelling in a safer form of transport.

Tucked in a foetal position, he tumbled over and over. His stomach churned, spewing acid into his oesophagus that spilled over into his burning mouth, as he bumped repeatedly against the sides of the damp hole, wishing he was somewhere else – far from this sickening, spiralling nightmare.

Just as he gave up all hope of surviving, he landed with a thump on a soft surface. Feeling nauseous, he breathed deeply. Had he survived the fall in one piece? Was he *dead*? He sniffed. Does death smell like…*leather*?

A sudden red light penetrated his eyelids. His eyes, glued together with fear, pinged open. A large red number ten had lit up on what looked like a dashboard. He blinked rapidly as his glassy, disorientated, eyes watched the swimming number ten change to nine.

'Frank!' He breathed deeply, trying to ease the lasting effects of motion sickness as the dashboard swayed in and out of focus like the camera of a paparazzi photographer on a speeding motorbike.

Frank climbed out of Wilmot's pocket, gripped a belt between his teeth, pulled it over Wilmot's shoulder and clicked it securely in place.

'What's happening, Frank?'

'Wilmot's imagination is now reality,' replied Frank, securing his own seatbelt.

Flashing from one number to the next the countdown continued: eight changed to seven, seven to six.

'I imagined myself in a car. Are we in a car?' Wilmot gasped.

Six changed to five.

Vibrations passed through his seat with the sudden roar of an engine.

Five changed to four.

The vehicle flew into reverse, throwing him forward in his seat. He slumped back, bumping his head, as the rest of the dashboard lit up.

'Three – two–' Frank counted along.

'The speedometer starts at zero and ends at the "speed of dark"!' cried Wilmot. 'How fast is that?' He'd heard of the 'speed of light' but not…

'Ooooone!' shouted Frank.

The car zoomed forward as if being fired from a giant catapult. Pinned to his seat, Wilmot could feel every organ push to the rear of his body, leaving him breathless. Wide-eyed, he stared at the speedometer, watching the needle gradually move to the halfway mark. Every small movement the needle made, the car went faster. He stamped his feet over the car floor, feeling for a brake pedal –

anything that might stop the car – but there were no pedals!

Spiralling through the darkness like a never-ending coil, Wilmot grappled with the steering wheel, bumping under the mercy of the hard suspension. Fighting for control, he tensed every aching arm muscle, but he was completely overpowered and unable to take control.

'Frank...are...you...okay?' he asked, straining to move his neck muscles against the incredible force.

There was no answer.

Eyes on the speedometer, Wilmot watched it flicker towards maximum speed: the 'speed of dark'. Losing focus, he stared at the dashboard lights fluttering like fairies before his eyes as the unbearable g-force continued to squeeze his body. He needed to stay awake. If he could just keep his eyes open a little longer. His eyelids dipped. The fairies turned into tiny dancing dots. Just a little longer...

Wilmot felt a diagonal strip of pressure against his chest as he jolted forward. Groaning, he opened his eyes to complete darkness and fell back in his seat. Had it all been a dream? Was he in his bedroom recovering from a nightmare? He tried to stand, but found he was still restrained in a seat. Wilmot could smell the leather interior of the car. Everything seemed too real to be a dream.

'Frank! Where are you?' He patted the seat next to him. His fingertips felt odd – numb – as if they'd been injected with an anaesthetic. 'Frank, answer me!'

Wilmot pressed the button to release his seatbelt and leaned forward to search for him. Unable to find Frank, he opened the door to activate the internal light. Splayed under the pedals was Frank's flattened body. The ridged imprint from the sole of Wilmot's shoe was stamped diagonally across his face.

'Oh no, Frank, what have I done?' Wilmot picked Frank up and puckered his lips to give him the kiss of life.

'Wilmot loves me! Wilmot gives me kisses!' said Frank, attempting a squashed-face grin. He blew out short puffs of air, gradually blowing up his cheeks, until he popped back to his usual shape without a single tread mark.

'You stupid idiot!' said Wilmot, spitting away any contamination and wiping his lips against the arm of his coat. 'AAAAAH!' He screamed as he dropped Frank on to his lap. 'What's happened to me? Where's my skin gone?' he exclaimed, turning his hands in front of his face.

'Frank told Wilmot he needs new skin.'

'My face!' His hands slid from his face to lift his pyjama top. 'I've no skin left anywhere! I'm a... *skeleton*!'

'Frank *tried* to give Wilmot all his new skin, so that he wouldn't have a shock when he arrived here.' Frank smiled. 'Wilmot has skin on legs.'

'Just my *legs*?' He pulled up his pyjama bottoms to check his legs. 'How can I go back to my normal life without any skin on the rest of my body?'

'Wilmot gets new skin soon.'

'My father's synthetic skin was all *destroyed* in the cellar! Without him to create more of it, I'll never have any, *you idiot*!'

'Wilmot's father makes more.'

'How can he make more skin – he's *dead*'?

'*Everyone's* dead in Madder's World.'

'My father – my *father* is in Madder's World?'

'Of course,' replied Frank. 'Madder's World is halfway place for all good people who die too young. Wilmot's father created special world.'

Wilmot stared, disbelievingly, at Frank. 'That's what he said – meet again in Madder's World!' said Wilmot, remembering part of his father's holographic message that now made sense. 'Am I *really* going to see my father again?'

'Frank thought Wilmot heard message.'

'No, I never heard all of it. Skin or no skin, I'll get to Madder's World now if it kills me.' He pushed the car door open, deliberately avoiding the next obvious question: was he dead already? Unable to cope with the answer to that yet, he stepped out of the car – finding his father was more important now.

Frank fell off his lap and plopped on to the soft muddy surface below.

'Is this place Madder's World?' asked Wilmot. Looking down both ends of the long desolate tunnel. He could see nothing but complete darkness at one end and a distant circle of light at the other. Drips of water fell from the blanket of blackness above, hitting the muddy ground in a chain of gentle plops. 'There's nothing here,' he added, looking up as he wiped away a droplet of cold water trickling down his skull.

'Wilmot, help!' yelled Frank, sinking into the mud. 'Help! Frank sinking!'

Wilmot leaned forward to pull Frank from the mud. 'Wow!' He gasped, dangling Frank's muddy body in mid air as he caught sight of the car he'd just driven. He couldn't believe it! He'd imagined travelling through the grave in a safer form of transport, but could this be true? Had he really travelled in a silver Aston-Martin DB5 – the magnificent 1960s classic sports car that James Bond had driven?

'I don't believe it! It's exactly the same as the car on one of my bedroom posters. How did I...?' Gobsmacked, he stared in awe at the streamlined silver bullet with its gleaming chrome wire wheels.

'Madder's World is made from lots of imaginary thoughts.'

'But–'

'Wilmot can use his imagination and turn it into reality.'

'How? I don't understand?' he asked. Walking round the car, with bulging eyes, he admired its sleek aerodynamic body – a full-sized version of his favourite car was actually standing right in front of him! 'This is unbelievable!'

'Fusion spray on Wilmot's legs helps Wilmot.'

'The fusion spray's enhanced my imagination?'

Frank nodded.

'So that's why my imagination has been so vivid. At least something is starting to make sense.'

Wilmot narrowed his eyes and looked down both ends of the dank tunnel. 'Which way do we go now? Do we head for the dark side or the circle of light at the other end?' he asked, studying the two distant ends. 'Shall we go the way the car's facing and head for the circle of light?' Wilmot turned on the spot. 'Where's the car? It's gone! The car's completely disappeared! Oh no! How will I ever get back home again?'

'If car is gone, Wilmot must've thought of something else?'

Wilmot knew exactly what the tunnel had reminded him of. A distant rumble echoed from the dark end of the tunnel. 'It can't be?' Vibrations shook the ground beneath his feet, rippling up his clattering skeletal body like sound waves pulsating through a rock concert amplifier. 'It is! Frank, we need to get out of the way!' he cried, flinging himself against the muddy tunnel wall.

Wilmot's imagination seemed out of control – more vivid than ever. The long tunnel had reminded him of the perilous scene from a spy film.

'Sorry, Frank!' he shouted, trying to be heard above the increasing noise of the approaching engine. 'I couldn't help it!'

Wilmot squeezed his eyes shut to try to delete the original thoughts of the film. But it was too late. The vibrations beneath his feet, thundering like a massive herd of approaching wildebeest, told him it was too late. A gust of wind whistled through the tunnel, passing through his skeletal head, almost knocking him over.

The engine chugged closer.

'Here it comes!'

CHAPTER SEVEN

The Inter-City train charged towards them like a determined bull. Bright front lights guided its way as the metal wheels rumbled over an invisible track.

Wilmot had no way of stopping it.

Pressed flat against the tunnel wall, his shoes wedged in the mud, Wilmot stood rigid. Clutching Frank safely to his chest, he readjusted his posture every time a gust of wind knocked him sideways.

The train got closer and closer. The wind grew stronger, gathering loose particles of mud to dance with as it blasted through the tunnel.

'Please – please miss us,' mumbled Wilmot. 'Hold on, Frank!' His toes curled like talons, gripping the insoles of his shoes.

In one huge blast, the train shot past at deafening speed. With the sudden loss of the lights at the front of the train, he was immediately plunged back into semi-darkness. Every window flickered in a seamless row of never-ending glass as he watched each carriage zoom past. But Wilmot knew that the train wasn't the only thing he'd imagined – there was something else in the tunnel following the train. Then he saw it, flying haphazardly through the tunnel behind the train.

The trailing helicopter swerved left then right, its rotor blades narrowly missing the tunnel walls.

Think. Think. What should he do next? Should he follow the train? *Would* he get to Madder's World and find his father if he didn't?

'Sorry, Frank, we've got to follow the train!' insisted Wilmot, stuffing him into his coat pocket.

Wilmot braced himself, focusing on the last carriage, waiting for the helicopter flying behind it. Wilmot's urge to see his father was too great.

The helicopter flew closer. Closer still.

Swooping dangerously low, the helicopter's rotor slowed, the individual blades slashing the air like ruthless battle swords, before regaining speed and disappearing into a whirling, circular blur.

Knees bent, Wilmot took a massive leap forward. Grasping cold metal with one hand, he found himself clinging to one of the helicopter's landing skids. The helicopter swerved sideways, its rotor whipping mud from the sidewall, as his weight unbalanced the already unstable machine. He dangled like an unstrung puppet until he finally managed to get a safer two-hand hold.

As the ground neared, Wilmot lifted his swaying legs and climbed upwards. Seconds later the engine misfired. Every bone in his body jolted as he fell back down. Wilmot reached up, grasping at the vibrating fuselage to try to pull himself back up, fighting the full force of the wind as the helicopter gradually increased speed. Wilmot knew he had to get to the front of the helicopter – he had to jump off it and on to the train before the end of the scene – before the helicopter *exploded* into a million pieces!

Clambering up the front of the unmanned machine, he reached out and grasped at or gained a foothold on any protrusion he could in order to slowly pull himself up the slippery fuselage. His painful cries were drowned out by the noise of the thunderous engine as he used all of his remaining strength to reach the front of the helicopter and turn to face the back of the train.

The wind blasted his eyeballs, drying them like a beached starfish, as his spine jolted up and down against the front of the helicopter. He squinted to look at the circle of light at the end of the tunnel appear over the bulk of the train and disappear again as the helicopter lost height. The long blades rotated above his head, blurring into one continuous circular saw, whirling like a single-minded executioner waiting to strike its victim. He held on to the sides of the fuselage, arms stretched back, fighting the relentless wind, waiting for the right moment. As the helicopter rose again, Wilmot got ready to jump.

'AAAAAH!' Wilmot screamed as he pushed forward, launching himself horizontally into the air.

At that moment, an enormous hot blast propelled him forward at awesome speed. His limbs rotated in the air until he finally hit the back of the train and held on like a limpet gripping a rock. He turned just in time to see the helicopter crash into the ground, reduced to a clunking metal fireball as it bounced through the tunnel. As the train pulled away, the bright heat of the flames slowly diminished until they resembled nothing more than the sparks from a match striking in the dark.

Wilmot's bones rattled against the vibrating bulk of metal as he held on with all his waning strength. The train continued to chug relentlessly for another thirty seconds, before a horrendous ear-splitting screech echoed through the tunnel and it gradually began to slow. Its engine groaned in protest of its strenuous journey, until it finally ground to a rumbling halt.

Wilmot released his grip and fell on to the soft, muddy ground below. 'I survived.' He rummaged around in his pocket, found Frank and pulled him out. 'Frank, are you all right?'

'Wilmot imagination bit *scary*.' Frank pulled his sock away from one of his hidden eyes.

'You're telling me – terrifying! I've watched *too* many films lately. That'll teach me to bunk off school.' He lifted himself from the mud, his ears buzzing from the noisy train resting beside him like a huge metal snake, and peered into the carriages for any sign of life. 'There's no one here – not a passenger in sight – they're all empty. It's just us, the train and a huge circular moon at the end of the tunnel.'

Continuing past the carriages, he headed towards the front of the train. Quite sure there were no other commuters on board, Wilmot's attention switched from the train to the strange circle of light. Its circumference was considerably larger now that he was so near. He stretched up, but the top of the circle was at least three metres above his fingertips. Mesmerized by its beautiful hazy glow, he moved closer to look through, curious as to what was on the other side, but it wasn't transparent.

'People are supposed to see a circle of light just before they die.' He paced up and down. 'The "*circle of death*", and I suppose I've got to go through it to get to Madder's World?' He sighed.

Frank nodded. 'Wilmot does.'

'How? Do I just *jump* through?' He continued to pace. 'Maybe I can drive the train through it?' He looked around. 'It's *gone*! Disappeared just like the car earlier. That's it then – there's no other way –

we'll have to jump.' Frank grinned an all-teeth grin back at him. 'Thanks, mate, you're a great help.'

Wilmot hesitated before making another move. 'Ready, Frank…unless, of course, you've any other suggestions?' Frank shook his head. He stepped one foot forward, bent both knees and focused ahead. 'In the words of Neil Armstrong – the first man on the Moon…' he said, as he ran forward and jumped straight into the circle of light with his eyes shut tight, 'one scary step for Wilmot…one giant leap for Fraaaaank!'

CHAPTER EIGHT

Wilmot felt a sense of weightlessness – light and buoyant – as if gravity had suddenly disappeared. He slowly opened one eye, and then the other.

Oh no! Panic! He was completely enclosed – trapped in a strange cumbersome suit with some sort of goldfish bowl on his head. He had to get it off! Wilmot tugged at the helmet with a growing sense of claustrophobia. But the task was made even more difficult by the oversized gloves he was now wearing. His breathing sounded weird, as if he were enclosed with an exhausted bear instead of his own heavy, laboured breath.

'Frank! Where are you? It – won't – come – off!' His voice sounded as if he'd swallowed an old transistor radio and it was transmitting his every word. No matter how hard he pulled – someone might as well have glued the damn thing to his head – there was no shifting it.

After several determined but unsuccessful tugs, he gave up and stared out at the desolate landscape before him. Turning with some difficulty in the stiff, bulky suit, he checked his surroundings. He was alone – completely isolated in a dusty barren environment pitted with holes. Some holes were massive: huge craters.

Had he actually landed on the Moon...wearing a spacesuit? No, Wilmot knew he couldn't have landed on the real Moon, not in the downward direction they had travelled to get to the tunnel, but it certainly looked real enough to him.

'Wow! Look at the stars!' he said, leaning back and gazing up at the glittering blackness. His eyes widened as something began to wriggle inside his spacesuit. 'Aliens! Frank! Help me! Where are you?' he cried, hitting his gloved hand against his chest to crush the thing squirming inside his suit. 'AAAAAH!'

Frank popped into Wilmot's helmet. 'Hello, Wilmot.'

'*Don't do that*...you scared the life out of me, you idiot! I'll *never* watch any of Mum's films again. I thought I'd got an alien trapped inside me.'

'Wilmot funny.' Frank sniggered.

'Really funny,' said Wilmot. "I haven't laughed this much in ages,' he added sarcastically.

Frank settled down in the corner of the helmet while Wilmot decided on his next move. Focusing on a row of pitted holes ahead, Wilmot pushed one leg forward, swung his opposite hip out and pushed the other leg forward. Before long he was gliding over the surface like an overweight ballerina, his every movement disturbing the sleeping moon-dust as he explored the unfamiliar landscape with Frank bobbing about inside his helmet.

Wilmot sighed. 'This can't be Madder's World. We're the only ones here.' He changed direction and headed for a crater the size of a family car. Teetering on its edge, Wilmot stared despondently at the huge dusty pit. 'There's no one here either, Frank.' He took a deep breath. 'I'll never find my father if all I do is create everything I see – cars, trains and now the moon – they all appear to be nothing but pointless figments of my own imagination!'

Then, something caught Wilmot's eye, glistening in the centre of the crater. He leaped forward, landed in the crater and bent down to pick it up. 'This is just like the box I found in your case in the cellar, Frank. I didn't imagine this here.' He tilted the box – the sound of chinking glass confirmed it also contained marbles – and caught a glimpse of his unfamiliar reflection (a skeleton head inside a bulbous space helmet) in the mirrored lid. 'It *must* belong to someone else. My imagination must have overlapped with someone else's imagination.' His eyes shifted to look at Frank inside his helmet. 'Is that how you meet people in Madder's World?'

Frank nodded. 'Wilmot meet people if they imagine same things as him.'

Wilmot checked the box over. 'Look! There's a name on the bottom. E – Eve Sparks. Do you know her, Frank?'

'Frank not know her,' he replied, shaking his head. 'She must like Moon too.'

'Sparks?' Wilmot thought fondly of his best friend Timothy Sparks. 'Well, I've never heard of her. She's definitely not from *my* imagination. Either she's here now or she's left her box behind.'

He looked up to check for any sign of life, but they were still alone.

Wilmot fumbled with the box's lid, hindered by his bulky gloves, until it clicked open to reveal several glass marbles. Some of them were totally transparent, while others appeared to be covered in unusual patterns that varied in colour. He carefully tipped the box over one of his gloved hands and waited for a marble to roll out.

Wilmot scrutinised its unusual white markings. 'It's moving – the image inside the marble is moving! Look – images of tiny moving people. Who are these people?' Frank clapped his hands against his cheeks and pursed his lips. 'Frank, what's the matter? You're turning…blue,' said Wilmot, moving his head to the back of his helmet so that Frank was in better focus.

With every passing second, Frank's cheeks puffed up a little more and his colour intensified. He was gradually expanding like an inflating blue balloon. Frank's concerned eyes stared straight at Wilmot, telling him, quite clearly, that he was unable to control the situation. Then, Frank let out a high-pitched squeal and began waving his arms in uncoordinated circles.

'Frank, what's the matter? Do I need to get you out?' Frank nodded. Frank's cheeks had expanded to such an extent now that Wilmot felt sure he'd explode at any moment. He yanked at his helmet. 'I'll never get the stupid thing off in time!'

Without care for his own safety, Wilmot ripped off his gloves and threw them to the ground. However, his bare skin didn't freeze in the lunar atmosphere. Instead, his hand felt warm as instant heat radiated from the marble. A vivid image of everything he'd seen inside the tiny marble suddenly filled his mind. He forgot about Frank and the helmet until…

Frank let out an enormous burp.

Seconds later, Wilmot was engulfed in a blinding flash of white light.

CHAPTER NINE

Wilmot hovered for a few seconds within the blinding light until he finally landed gently on solid ground.

'*Disgusting*!' he protested. Long, thick globules of clear liquid dripped from his bony face on to his coat – his spacesuit had disappeared. 'Frank! You burped all over me, *you idiot*!'

As soon as he lifted his dripping head, Wilmot realised he was no longer on the Moon. He was standing in the middle of a huge, white room bustling with life. The walls were white, the ceiling was blinding white, dotted with hundreds of small glaring spotlights, and the floor was covered with a shiny white marble-like substance. The hum of voices mixed with shuffling and tapping footsteps filled the vibrant room.

Flicking a stringy globule of expelled fusion spray from his chin, he turned on the spot to look at the whole room. Where was he now? This place reminded him of a departure lounge in an airport.

But there was one fundamental difference – some of these holidaymakers were skeletons just like Wilmot!

Frank pulled at Wilmot's pyjama bottoms. 'There you are,' he said, bending down to pick him up. Frank had changed back to his usual pale yellow colour and shape. 'Am I inside Eve Sparks' marble – inside the image I saw?'

Frank nodded.

'This is amazing!' He wiped away a loop of fusion spray that hung like snot from his nose. 'It must have happened when I held the marble,' he said, opening one hand to reveal the marble, still warm against his skin, and the other holding the small box. He placed the marble safely inside the box.

'Muckers unite!' shouted some of the people at the back of the room. 'Muckers unite!' More and more people began to join in. 'Muckers unite!'

Wilmot's bones locked into a rigid upright position as he scanned the large room like a meerkat on lookout duty, observing the sudden change in atmosphere. A few tense moments followed, before hundreds of small balls were launched into the air, hurtling in mass over Wilmot's head.

'Frank, what's happening?' Wilmot ducked, narrowly avoiding a direct hit from one of the balls.

Suck! Suck! Suck! Suck!

Frank turned himself into a ball.

'What are you *doing*? Don't hide now!'

'Kick him! We need all the help we can get!' said a voice from behind Wilmot. A teenage girl slid in front of him on her roller blades. 'Copy me.' She kicked her ball into the air. 'Do it – *quickly*!'

Flabbergasted, he stared at the girl as if she were mad. Before he had a chance to stop her, she snatched Frank from his grasp and booted him into the air. Then, she took hold of Wilmot's bony hand and proceeded to drag him to the back of the room.

'What did you do that for? I'll never find him again?' exclaimed Wilmot, trying to be heard above the noisy chants.

'Muckers unite! Muckers unite!'

Wilmot desperately tried to free himself from her grip, as she continued gliding across the shiny floor on her roller blades. The more he pulled, the more she tightened her hold, digging her nails into his bones, refusing to let go.

'Where are we going?' he protested, getting a mouthful of her whipping ginger hair and spitting it back out again.

'There's no time to explain – just follow me!'

Once they'd reached the farthest corner of the room, she stopped suddenly. Colliding straight into her, his bones clattering like a tuneless xylophone, Wilmot quickly regained balance and turned round.

Everyone had congregated on this side of the room except for one skeleton, dressed in male clothing, left standing alone in the centre. Mucker balls were bouncing in every direction, careering off the walls and hitting the floor, just like Frank when he'd destroyed the cellar at home.

Then, almost as quickly as they had started, the muckers stopped bouncing and gathered (side-by-side and one on top of the other) to form a huge wall of balls held together like a colossal ant bivouac protecting its vulnerable queen. This impenetrable barrier moved forward in unison, as it continued to push the lone skeleton to the opposite end of the room.

'What's happening?' asked Wilmot.

'There's someone here who shouldn't be here,' informed the girl. 'The muckers will get rid of him.'

Pushed to the last strip of space, the skeleton darted up and down. Trapped, the skeleton fell to his knees. 'Help me!' he shouted. 'Someone help me!' Sobbing, he held his head in his hands.

'We've got to help him!' insisted Wilmot, moving forward. Several hands grasped his coat, pulling him back. 'Let me go! What are they doing to him?' he asked, pulling until his coat fabric was unable to stretch further.

Suddenly, the mucker balls dropped to the floor and began to roll away from the kneeling skeleton. Seconds later, the back wall of the large room flipped open like a giant box and the skeleton was sucked from the room into the dark void beyond.

A chilly breeze swept through the room, blowing every mucker across the floor like tumbleweed in a spaghetti western, as the skeleton's body drifted peacefully, circling with outstretched limbs, into oblivion. When he was nothing more than a small spinning dot in the distance, the wall finally lifted, shutting the giant box, leaving no sign that the skeleton had ever been there.

The people holding Wilmot released their grip. '*Thank you*,' he muttered, rearranging his coat so that it was no longer hanging halfway down his back. 'Who was that, and where has he gone?' Wilmot asked the girl.

About the same age as him, she was slimly built with long, curly ginger hair and a kind smile. Her nose was dotted with pretty light-brown freckles, enhanced by the glow from her bright orange tracksuit-top worn with some less vibrant blue leggings.

'No one knows – nobody ever finds out,' she answered. 'But there's one thing you can be sure of, if he's not welcome in Madder's World, he must have done something *very* bad before he died.'

'Like what…*murder*?'

'Your guess is as good as mine.' She shrugged. 'Only *good* people who die young are allowed to live out their remaining years in Madder's World.'

'How can you tell whether someone is good or bad?'

'If a person is evil they'll have a black heart, of course. By the way, my name's Lunetta Miles.'

'I'm Wilmot.'

Lunetta smiled. 'Welcome to Madder's World, Wilmot.' She turned round smoothly on her roller blades and began to meander between the crowds of people beginning to resume their usual business. 'As a newcomer I knew you wouldn't know what to do with your mucker,' she said, turning to look at him.

Jogging behind, he tried to keep up. 'How–'

'The lack of skin's a bit of a giveaway.' Lunetta laughed. 'That's how we find out whether or not someone has a black heart – because there's no chest skin to hide the heart.'

'Oh, I'd forgotten about my skin – or lack of it.' Wilmot lowered his head, feeling almost naked knowing she'd got her skin and he hadn't. How stupid did he look – the lack of skin would obviously make it much easier to detect someone with a black heart. He lifted his pyjama top and sighed with relief – his heart was still red.

'Don't worry; we'll sort out your skin in a minute. But before we go anywhere, we need to find our muckers.'

'Does *everyone* here have a mucker?'

'Of course, they protect us from intruders – from anyone who shouldn't be here.' She stopped and looked from one transforming mucker to the next.

'Where are we?' asked Wilmot.

'You're in the Waiting Room. It's the first place you visit when you arrive in Madder's World. It's where you get your new skin.'

'Did William Madder give you your skin? Do you know where I can find him? I'm his son. I'm Wilmot Madder,' he said, scarcely stopping for breath.

'William Madder's *your* father?'

'Yes, do you know where I can find him?'

'I know of him, because he created this place. But I've never met him,' she replied, sadly.

Wilmot sighed. 'I have to find him before my mother realises I've left the real world. I don't know how to get back home without him.'

She gasped. 'You'll *never* be able to leave. Accept it, you're *dead* like the rest of us.' She lifted her T-shirt. 'Look at your heart, just like mine and everyone else here, you'll find it's stopped beating.'

'*Dead*! You're *dead*! I'm not – I – I can't be dead.' He looked through her ribcage. 'You've got no torso skin. I can see your heart, and it's... stopped beating.' He lifted his pyjama top. 'But my heart *is* still beating. So, that must mean I'm *not* dead!'

'That's weird.' She frowned. 'Maybe you *are* still alive. However, I've heard that one day we'll all have beating hearts again.'

'I can't believe this...you're dead. I'm actually talking to a...*dead person*!' he exclaimed, his voice rising to a high-pitched incoherent squeal at the end of his sentence. He paused to compose himself and adjust the tone of his voice. 'If you're no longer alive, why do you need a beating heart?'

'Rumour has it that it's the only way for us to know when to leave Madder's World. The heart should apparently act as a clock, to let us know when our expected life span would have ended naturally in the real world, so that when our time is up we can leave and join our loved-ones in heaven – or wherever else you might go when you die of old age.' She stared at Wilmot's fixed gaze. 'Are you...okay?'

He blinked. 'Yes...this is all very–'

'Surreal?' interjected Lunetta.

'Yes, unbelievably dreamlike.' Wilmot paused momentarily before asking, 'How did you die?'

'I don't remember much. I was roller blading, I fell, and when I woke up I was in a dark tunnel running towards a circle of light.' A more feminine, daintier replica of Frank came waddling towards her wearing a red and white polka dot neckerchief, wrapped round her middle and tied in a neat bow just beneath her mouth. 'Hello, Lily!' Her eyes were almond shaped, compared to Frank's rounder eyes, and her mouth appeared fractionally smaller, which made her look less mischievous.

Lunetta's mucker reminded Wilmot of a photograph of his mother and father displayed on the living room mantelpiece at home: his mother had worn an identical spotty neckerchief.

'This is unbelievable! I thought Frank was the only one of his kind, but there are literally hundreds of them!' He leaned forward. 'Hello, Lily, do you know Frank?'

Lily pointed at a group of muckers transforming back from their ball-like state. Looking from one to the next, Wilmot tried to spot Frank's distinctive orange and white striped sock. But most of the muckers seemed to be wearing at least one item of clothing: the majority had brightly coloured socks like Frank, but some – probably females – were wearing neckerchiefs tied round their heads or their middles, which made them look like partially wrapped mechanical toys on demonstration in a hectic toyshop as they tottered around suffering from the dizzy side-effects of their recent bounce.

'There he is!' said Wilmot. Frank waddled over – with his wrinkled, inside-out sock hanging from one side of his head – and grinned. 'What *do* you look like?' Wilmot laughed and bent down to pick him up. He pulled Frank's sock off and turned it the right way before placing it back on his head.

'I could say the same about you,' said Lunetta, grinning at Wilmot. 'He got you then?'

'Got me?'

'You're covered in...' She paused to giggle. 'You're covered in mucker wee.'

'Terrific! It's nice to know I've been urinated on!' he said, brushing another globule of expelled fusion spray from his coat. 'Thanks, Frank. I suppose I should have guessed your big burping mouth would make up for having no holes anywhere else.'

'Frank really sorry.' Smiling mischievously, he squeezed through Wilmot's grip and plopped to the floor where he joined Lily and held her hand.

'It happens to all of us eventually,' admitted Lunetta, smirking. 'Keep your distance the next time he starts to turn blue. Follow me – I think it's time for you to line up for some new skin.'

Wilmot followed Lunetta to the back of a short queue in front of some strange suspended dust, forming shapes that resembled human outlines.

'Good evening,' said the dusty figure, turning to address him with a nod. The dust spread slightly, distorting the figure, before reforming again.

'Hello,' replied Wilmot, his voice quivery. He waited for him to turn round. 'Who–' he whispered.

'Oh, they're cremated people – people who are burnt after death,' she whispered back.

'How can *they* get new skin when there's no bone for it to attach to?'

'The new skin combines with any form of DNA – even ash.'

'Oh,' replied Wilmot. He asked nothing more. If he could accept talking freely to a dead person, he could definitely accept this explanation – even if he didn't understand it.

When he finally reached the front of the queue, he prised Frank away from Lily and followed an overweight lady through a set of double doors. 'Will you wait for me to come out?'

'I'll wait at the exit! But it won't be easy to recognise you with your skin!' said Lunetta.

'Don't worry – I'll find you!' he said, as the doors closed behind him.

CHAPTER TEN

On the other side of the doors, Wilmot found himself in a long thin room. A row of seated people, all at various stages of receiving their new skin, stretched along the entire length of the room like a weird factory production line for plastic surgery: some had their arm skin, others their legs and arms, while a few had reached the final stage and were receiving their new head skin. Behind them were various benches containing numerous colourful, bubbling vials and test tubes – just like those he'd discovered in the cellar.

Wilmot followed the short, overweight woman, her bottom bouncing like two trapped cushions beneath her skirt, as she moved from one person to the next checking the progress of each individual. 'This one's free,' she said, waving her clipboard. She hurried off, tights rasping between her chubby legs, leaving him in the hands of one of her colleagues.

After a quick visual examination, the podgy man – wearing a tight, white lab coat with about fifty pens jammed in his top pocket – told Wilmot to remove all items of clothing except his underwear. Realising Wilmot already had his new leg skin, the man quickly moved on to his arm skin, which he retrieved with a long pair of tweezers from a vial containing green liquid behind him.

Wilmot braced himself for the tickling sensation he'd experienced last time. But as soon as the fusion spray was administered, his new arm skin shrank and attached to his bone without irritating him. In fact, it felt warm and soothing, leaving him thankful he'd waited to get the rest of his new skin as it seemed much less of an ordeal now that he'd no sensitive skin for it to attach to.

As Wilmot sat patiently waiting for his new skin to be sprayed, Frank hovered around Wilmot's chair. As soon as spraying commenced, he began scavenging every tiny droplet of fusion spray that landed near him, almost wearing his tongue out, licking every surface it landed on thoroughly clean. Wilmot knew, with that much liquid inside him, he'd have to watch Frank carefully for any sign of a pending burp.

Last of all, Wilmot waited for his new head and face skin. The man seemed far too involved in his work – just like everyone else in this part of the waiting room – to ask him whether he knew his father. In any case, before Wilmot could speak, a huge head was plonked over his face like a giant Halloween mask.

Once the process was complete, Wilmot touched his face. His fingers no longer a numb skeleton, he felt the contours of his new skin. 'Amazing! I've even got my hair back!' he said, sliding his fingers through his new hair, which felt as thick and out of control as always.

'Next!' called the man, eager to proceed.

Wilmot got up and another person was instantly seated in his chair.

'Wilmot!' said Frank, smiling. 'Wilmot looks like Wilmot again.'

'Time for us to leave, Frank,' he said, pulling his pyjama top over his head. As soon as he was dressed, he picked Frank up and moved on through a dimly lit, white corridor. 'Urgh! You're all sticky.'

Frank licked his lips. 'Frank had lots of fusion spray. Frank collected some sticky spray on arms to eat later.'

'Just warn me earlier than last time if you need to burp – okay?'

Frank nodded with a wry grin.

Wilmot was encouraged to move forward by the small queue forming behind him. He continued down the gradually widening corridor until he reached a group of people congregated at the far end who were slowly diverging into two separate rooms. However, as soon as it was realised he'd already got a mucker and a reflection box, he was directed through a set of double doors that led back into the intense brightness of the Waiting Room.

Squinting, he looked around the busy room. 'Lunetta!'

'Lily!' called Frank, spotting her rushing towards him. 'Look what Frank collected for you,' he said, extending his thin, sticky arms out towards her.

'Ooh, yummy!' she said, poking out her tongue and licking the excess spray directly off his arms.

'So that's what you look like,' said Lunetta, skating over to him. 'You're quite different to how I'd expected you to look.'

'Not uglier I hope.'

'No, just different.' Lunetta blushed. She spotted the tiny box in Wilmot's hand. 'I see they've given you your reflection box.'

'Actually, it's not mine. They didn't give me my own box when they noticed I already had one. I found this one on the Moon. Do you know anyone called Eve Sparks?' he asked, showing her the tiny box.

'Yes, I do. You must have visited *my* Moon – it's a special place I created here in Madder's World. We use the marbles in our reflection box to create new places to live in and to travel from one place to the next. I was with Eve and her brother, Timothy, on my Moon the other day. She must have left her reflection box there.'

'*Timothy?*' It can't be…the Timothy he knew didn't have a sister. 'You know a Timothy Sparks?'

'Yes, he's Eve Sparks' brother. Do you know Timothy too?' asked Lunetta. 'He's newly arrived. He got killed by a car outside his school.'

Wilmot gasped. 'My best friend Timothy got killed by a car. But it can't be him, because he never had a sister.'

'We could find out if it is him. All we need to do is look inside Eve's reflection box to find out which marble is missing. Once we know where she is, we can try to find her. She'll know where to find Timothy, and then you can find out if her brother's *your* Timothy Sparks.'

'I don't understand. If the marble's missing then how–?'

'She might be able to tell you where you can find your father too,' she continued, excitedly. 'Eve's been in Madder's World longer than anyone else I know. She died more than six years ago.' Lunetta held out her hand. 'May I look in her reflection box?' Lunetta took the box and sifted through. 'She's in her bedroom! The marble containing the image of her bedroom is the only missing marble.'

'But how can we get to her bedroom without that particular marble?'

'When we first receive a reflection box, we are all given ten empty marbles that we can fill with ten special images – places that you can actually visit. Each marble can be filled with any place you've ever wished to create or visit – limited only by your own imagination. Once you've filled one of the marbles, you can take a friend or relative to your special place with you. All you have to do is get them to look at the image inside the marble, and then, if they want to share it with you, they hold the marble with you and off you both go. Or, alternatively, they can fill one of their own marbles with the same image, so that they can go there whenever they want.'

'But–' interrupted Wilmot.

'Guess who has a marble with a copy of Eve's bedroom?' She smiled. 'Me! We can go there now, if you'd like to go with me?'

'What if he isn't the Timothy I know?'

'Even if he isn't, Eve might still be able to help you find your father because she knows more people here than anyone else I know.' Lunetta pulled her reflection box from her tracksuit-top pocket and opened it. 'Here it is.'

Wilmot stared at the marble. 'It looks like a room for a...baby.'

'She *was* very young when she died.'

'Is she still a baby now?'

'No, she's almost eight.' She smiled. 'We still get older here.'

'You still get *older*? If you can't leave Madder's World how...you can't continue ageing for ever and ever – can you?'

Lunetta frowned. 'I – I don't know.'

It was quite obvious she'd never given the matter any thought before now. 'I'd love to meet Eve,' said Wilmot, quickly changing the subject.

Lunetta's worried expression reverted to a smile. 'I'm sure she'd love to meet you too. Now, think of Eve's room, hold my hand and the marble will warm between our palms.'

Wilmot scooped up Frank and Lily. He passed Lunetta her mucker before taking her hand and shutting his eyes. The small marble warmed instantaneously between their palms. His mind filled with the vivid image of Eve's room as a blinding light penetrated his crimson eyelids. He squeezed his eyes tightly together. Seconds later, his feet lifted from the floor. Unsupported, as if suspended upright on an invisible harness, his body rocked in mid-air.

Finally, Wilmot landed and opened his eyes. His feet gradually sank into a soft, cream carpet. The long pile covered his shoes like deep fluffy snow.

Wilmot gazed up at the huge furniture. 'I've shrunk!'

'You haven't got smaller, quite the opposite, everything else has got bigger,' informed Lunetta. She let go of his hand and knelt down on one knee. 'I've just got to get these roller blades off – they're useless here. Whatever you do don't put Frank down because it's a total nightmare trying to find a mucker in this carpet.'

Frank's bottom lip protruded sulkily.

Breathing in the pleasant smell of talcum powder and freshly washed linen, Wilmot scanned the pale yellow room. 'Is she here? I can't see anyone.'

Wilmot moved forward, shuffling through the carpet and flattening its fluffy surface, heading for an enormous cot on the far side of the room. Standing on tiptoes, he peered inside – nothing but puppy-decorated bedding. He looked up at a large rectangular window high on the wall above, draped with matching puppy-embroidered cotton curtains, knowing that, like almost everything else in the room, it was out of reach.

Beside the cot stood a massive white wardrobe with handles as big as a heavyweight boxer's fists. Several large toy dogs flopped over the top. Each one seemed to be staring at him as if ready to pounce at any moment. Faint music played in the background. The muffled tune seemed familiar: although he couldn't quite place it, he knew it was a Christmas song.

Frank lowered himself deeper into Wilmot's pocket. 'Why is everything so big? Is Eve *giant* baby?' He peered out of the pocket, eyeballs rotating, and scanned the room.

'I know why! This is how Eve's room would have looked from her perspective, before she died, because everything looks much bigger when you're really young.'

'You're right, it's how Eve viewed the real world before she died,' added Lunetta, placing a roller blade under each armpit.

Wilmot's eyes were suddenly drawn to a photo frame on a chest of drawers beside the cot. He stretched up and only just managed to reach it. Although he was unable to make out the finer details of the blurred image, Wilmot could see the figure of a man holding a small boy on his shoulders with his arm around the waist of a woman standing beside him. It had to be a photo of her brother, Timothy, and her parents. But she hadn't remembered their faces clearly enough for Wilmot to recognise any of them.

'Please, put that down,' said someone behind him.

Wilmot turned sharply, almost dropping the photo frame, to face a young girl wearing a white cotton nightdress with wispy blonde hair and piercing blue eyes.

'Who are you?' she asked, wrinkling her little nose.

'Oh – sorry – I'm Wilmot,' he answered, 'a friend…of Lunetta's.'

'I'm Eve. It's nice to meet you,' she said, holding the sides of her nightdress and giving him a little curtsey.

'Hello, Eve,' said Lunetta. She reached for a sword, dwarfed by the wardrobe it had been leaning against, and picked it up. 'Did you forget this?'

'Lunetta!' Eve took the sword. 'I had no idea you were here.' She wrapped her arms around Lunetta.

'Have you lost anything else lately?' Lunetta asked. She smiled discreetly at Wilmot.

Wilmot took the hint and began rummaging in his pocket. 'I think this is your reflection box,' he said, passing it to Eve.

'Brilliant! Where did you find it?' she asked, releasing Lunetta and reaching for her precious little box.

'You left it on the Moon,' informed Lunetta.

'Thank you, I'd lose my head if it wasn't screwed on properly,' said Eve, retrieving the missing marble, containing the image of her bedroom, from her nightdress pocket and placing it safely back inside her reflection box.

'I'm sorry to be rude, having only just met you, but I have to go – Timothy needs my help.' She lifted the sword to waist height, looked down the blade and nodded approvingly before slicing the air.

'We'll come with you,' said Lunetta. 'Wilmot would like to meet your brother.'

'Brilliant! We need all the help we can get,' said Eve. 'This is where we've got to go.' She opened her hand to show Wilmot another marble. 'I borrowed it from Timothy, so that I can get back to him with my sword. And one for you,' she said, passing Lunetta a marble containing the same image from her reflection box.

'I'm not going in there!' exclaimed Wilmot. 'I'll be dead within two minutes. They'll kill me!'

'Don't be silly – you're *already* dead,' said Eve.

Before Wilmot had time to speak again, Eve grabbed his hand. The marble, held between their palms, began to warm. 'Please, I – I don't think I'm deeeeead!' cried Wilmot, as a blinding light flashed before his eyes.

CHAPTER ELEVEN

Before Wilmot's eyes had adjusted to his new surroundings, his arm fell like a lead weight in front of him: the heavy sword he was holding had spiked the ground, narrowly missing his black leather boots – he was wearing *knee-high boots*!

'Just in time for the action, girls!' said a boy behind Wilmot.

'Timothy?'

Wilmot looked up. He was standing in a remote farmyard, between two large dilapidated barns, dotted with chickens clucking and pecking at the dusty ground. His eyes followed some strangely dressed men, wearing tunics and large feathered hats, beginning to form a circle around them. Instinctively, he lifted his sword. Who were these men, and why were they looking so…*angry*?

Small beads of sweat bubbled like pimples on his forehead under the heavy, oversized black hat he was now wearing. Pushing the wide brim away from his eyes, he began to slowly move in a back-to-back circle with the others.

'Timothy, is it you?' asked Wilmot. He looked over his shoulder but was unable to distinguish boy from girl under the three hats at varying heights behind him – they, too, were all clothed in the same fancy attire he was wearing.

'Attack!' shouted one of the men surrounding them, lifting his sword in the air.

'No! Don't attack!' cried Wilmot, turning to face them. His eyes darted from left to right, checking for a safe escape route.

Brandishing their swords, the men came charging at them from every angle. Startled chickens flew, wings flapping violently, in all directions.

'All for one and one for all!' shouted Lunetta, Eve and the boy.

'No!' exclaimed Wilmot, tightening his sweaty grip on the heavy sword. 'I've never even held a real sword before!'

One man charged forward with his sword pointing straight at him like a soldier with a bayonet at the forefront of battle. Wilmot sliced the air with his sword, forcing every tense muscle in his arms to follow his command, to try to intimidate the angry man.

CLANG! The two swords clashed. Wilmot felt the vibrations pass through the ends of his tingling fingers and up his arms. Without a moment to spare, he swung his sword back and thrust his entire bodyweight into his next swing. Skidding on the dusty gravel, he missed his opponent's sword and turned back round, quickly regaining his balance to defend a powerful blow aimed at his head. He pushed forward, holding his sword horizontally against his attacker's sword, forcing him successfully to the ground.

'Frank!' Wilmot cried, as the attacker booted his shin. He staggered backwards on the dusty ground, watching Frank run in the opposite direction to the safety of one of the nearby barns. 'Frank, help me!'

Within seconds, the man scrambled to his feet and headed straight for him. Wilmot struck the bearded man's chest, ripping his fancy tunic with a diagonal slash. Without stopping, the man lunged at him again, but Wilmot ducked and scuffled sideways, dodging a second blow aimed at his head. He heard his opponent's sword smack the ground, the force still churning up the dust as Wilmot turned and regained his composure. The man adjusted his stance, dragged his heavy sword across the earth and pointed its gleaming blade back in Wilmot's direction.

Knees bent, Wilmot moved from one side to the next, thrashing his sword in uncoordinated movements to try to outwit his opponent. The man copied Wilmot, as if they were engaged in some kind of tribal dance, swiping his sword at every available opportunity.

Suddenly, Wilmot felt a piercing blow to his arm. His arm felt warm and wet: the fancy sleeve of his white shirt had been sliced open and his arm was bleeding. He glared at the crazed man before him and tightened his grip on the sword. Every muscle in his body tensed like a compressed spring waiting to uncoil as he focused on his opponent's torso. He had to end the fight before this man killed him – assuming, of course, he wasn't *dead* already!

Wilmot waited for the right moment, lunged forward and thrust his sword into the man's chest. The injured man staggered momentarily before falling to the floor. 'Oh no!' Wilmot gasped. 'What have I done?' He pulled the sword, which slid out with amazing ease, from the man's chest and stepped back. Seconds later, the man's body disappeared, leaving nothing but his clothes.

Wilmot rushed forward. He picked up the dead man's sword, lying on top of his clothes, and lifted each empty garment before dropping them to the ground. His body had completely vanished.

THUMP! Another body fell next to the dead man's clothes. Within seconds, the second man also disappeared. Now there were two lifeless piles of clothes at his feet.

'Got him!' said Lunetta, bending down to take her opponent's sword. She ran off and charged fearlessly into a group of three men fighting the other boy.

'Timothy?' Wilmot said to himself. He was still unable to see the boy's face beneath his tilted feather hat.

'AAAAAH!' cried another maniac, leaping straight at Wilmot.

Wilmot used the first attacker's sword with his own, crossing them together above his head, to block the blow aimed at his skull. He kicked out, eventually giving the man a severe boot in the groin, which caused him to buckle and fall to the ground. But the man quickly got to his feet like a determined android programmed to kill and came charging back towards him.

Wilmot shut his eyes and prayed for the nightmare to end. He could hear the man's approaching footsteps getting closer. Closer still. Without a moment to spare, Wilmot opened his eyes and sliced his two swords diagonally in the air at head height. The dead man's head fell to the ground with a thud and rolled across the ground. His body buckled like a leaning sack of potatoes before falling to the ground in a cloud of dust directly in front of him. Then, just like the other men, the head and the body disappeared, leaving nothing but a hat separated from the rest of his empty clothes.

Wilmot panted heavily as he looked around for the next possible attacker. The enemy numbers were dwindling fast: replaced by piles of lifeless clothes. Then, Wilmot spotted Eve in trouble and ran to her aid. Before he could help, she stabbed her attacker and left his injured body to fall to the ground. Within seconds, he vanished just like all the others.

Wilmot heard swords clashing. He turned in the direction of the sound and quickly rushed forward, scattering the dead men's clothes as he kicked them out of his way, and headed for the boy still fighting the last of the men. 'Timothy!'

'Wilmot?' said the boy, stopping mid-fight. His mouth gaped open. Grasping the sword piercing his unguarded chest, he arched forward and fell to his knees.

Lunetta jumped over the fallen clothes, thrust her sword into the back of the man who had just stabbed Timothy and finished the battle.

'Timothy!' cried Wilmot, dropping to his knees next to him. He placed his arms around his best friend's shoulders and lifted his injured upper body from the ground. 'What have I done?'

CHAPTER TWELVE

Timothy's limp body rested on Wilmot's lap, his hat lopped to one side revealing his short mousy-brown hair. 'Timothy, don't die. Please, don't die!' His arm felt numb under the weight of his friend's larger frame.

Lunetta cleared her throat. 'Wilmot,' she said softly, 'he's–'

Timothy's body jerked forward. 'I'm already dead!' he said, opening his eyes. 'I deserve an Oscar for that!'

The two girls giggled.

Wilmot helped Timothy to his feet. 'You're okay? But you were stabbed…'

'No harm done.' Timothy pulled the sword from his skinless chest and threw it to the floor. 'I can't believe you're here!'

'He *is* the same Timothy!' said Lunetta.

'You know each other?' asked Eve.

Timothy placed his arm around Wilmot's shoulder. 'This is my best mate.' His chubby cheeks bunched up, reducing his eyes to slits, as he smiled. 'Our fourth Musketeer!'

'The sword fight was all for *fun*?' Wilmot frowned.

'The best fight I've had in ages! What a *wonderful* imagination I have,' he added, nudging Wilmot.

Wilmot beamed at Timothy. 'I can't believe it's you…right here beside me. Life's been really awful without you. Seeing you again is like a dream come true.'

'I'm sorry, mate. The mental driver came out of nowhere – I didn't have a chance.'

'The story was reported in all the newspapers. A man called David Fuller was driving the car,' informed Wilmot. 'He's been caught drink-driving several times before. So, the police think he was probably drunk when he hit you. He knocked over and injured an old man who lives opposite the school without stopping a few weeks before your accident. Apparently, he wasn't badly hurt – just a few painful bruises – but he'd been looking out for the car that'd hit him ever since. Keeping an eye on

127

the road during busy periods, he'd witnessed the same car fleeing the scene of your accident and called the ambulance.'

'I hope this David Fuller's been locked up for life!' said Eve.

Wilmot lowered his head. 'They found his abandoned car but they haven't caught him yet. The police reckon he's hiding somewhere. They'll catch him eventually – he can't hide forever.'

'How did *you* die?' asked Timothy. 'I certainly didn't expect to see you here.'

'I'm not technically dead – well, at least I don't think I am.'

'Not *dead*?' exclaimed Eve. 'But *everyone* is dead here. You've just been in a sword fight. Are you *mad*!'

'I'm Madder,' said Wilmot, with a wry grin. 'That reminds me,' – feeling his left arm – 'I was injured in the fight.' Pulling back the torn, bloodstained fabric of his shirt, he searched for the wound. 'I'm sure I–'

'Your synthetic skin would have healed by now. It only takes a few minutes for it to return to normal,' informed Timothy. 'We couldn't do half the things we do here without this amazing skin.'

'Wilmot has got synthetic skin,' said Lunetta, 'but he's not completely the same as the rest of us. He has a beating heart, *and* he says he's "Madder" because Wilmot is William Madder's son.'

'I know,' said Timothy. 'Your father came to see me in the waiting room when I first came to Madder's World.'

Wilmot's eyes widened. 'You've actually spoken to him?'

'He asked me a million questions about you.'

'Where is he now? I can't wait to see him.'

Timothy hesitated. 'I – I don't know.'

'You don't know?'

Timothy shook his head.

Wilmot turned to speak to Eve. 'Do *you* know where I can find him?'

Biting her bottom lip, she shook her head too.

Wilmot sighed. 'Oh no, I've come this far and I'm *still* no closer to finding him.'

'Your dad is probably waiting for your image to appear on the mirrored lid of his reflection box,' said Lunetta, attracting Wilmot's full attention. 'An image appears when a loved-one dies, so that you know when to go to the waiting room and meet them.'

'But if Wilmot isn't dead, his image won't appear on his father's reflection box,' added Timothy.

Eve turned to speak to Timothy. 'I never came to meet you. I saw your image on my reflection box, but I didn't recognise you as my brother because I died too young to remember you properly. But you still found me.'

'I never knew you had a sister,' said Wilmot.

'Mum didn't like me to talk about Eve's death, so I didn't tell anyone. That's why the spare bedroom was always locked; it was Eve's room before she died. Mum kept, and probably still keeps, the room like a shrine. Since her death, no one has been allowed to enter or touch anything. When I grew taller, I used to unlock her room and go in when Mum wasn't at home. It's a good thing I did because I'd never have found Eve otherwise.'

'So how did you find Eve?' asked Wilmot, puzzled.

'I put the image of her bedroom into one of my marbles and our imaginary places overlapped,' replied Timothy.

Lunetta laughed. 'Most of your imagination.'

'I don't remember finding spare swords in my room before *you* got here,' added Eve.

'Okay, maybe I made a few *minor* alterations.' Timothy laughed.

'That's it!' said Wilmot. 'Dad might be living in a room identical to one in my house, right here in Madder's World. And if my guess is correct, he'll have recreated the place where he carried out all his experiments: the cellar! If I do the same as you, but put the image of Dad's cellar inside a marble, my imagination might overlap with my father's imagination and I'll find him!'

'Well, it worked for Timothy,' said Lunetta. 'Would you like to use one of my unused marbles?' She opened her reflection box, searched for a clear marble and passed it to Wilmot. 'You'd better find Frank before you leave though. You can't go anywhere without him.' She looked around. 'Lily!'

'Johnny!' called Timothy.

'Gemmy!' called Eve.

Wilmot laughed. 'You've all got a mucker – this is amazing! Frank must think he's in mucker heaven. I saw him running into that barn,' – he points – 'maybe they're all in there together.'

Wilmot jumped over the piles of clothes and headed to the barn, followed by the others, his sword clanking at his side.

'Frank!' called Wilmot, shuffling his boots through the layers of dry straw on the barn floor to see if he was hiding beneath it.

The decrepit barn contained nothing but a few broken bales scattered at its rear with a central ladder that led up to a small hayloft. Although uninhabited, the barn reeked with the pungent scent of animal urine and dung, permeating the stale air.

'Urgh! It stinks of...horse poo in here. Frank, where are you?' he yelled, pinching his nostrils together as his feet continued to stir up the foul smell.

'We're up here!' shouted a thicker-set mucker wearing no clothes.

Timothy clambered up the hayloft ladder. 'Hello, Johnny, what are you doing up here, my old mate?'

'Is Frank up there?' asked Wilmot.

'You must come quickly!' yelled another female mucker, standing next to Lily, wearing a pink and white flowered sock on her head.

'Gemmy, what are you doing?' asked Eve, placing her foot on the bottom rung.

'Something's scared Frank!' shouted Timothy.

'Brilliant,' said Wilmot, sarcastically, following Eve up the rickety ladder. 'Frank, stop messing about. I think I've worked out how to find Dad.' When he reached the top, Wilmot found Frank shaking on a hay bale. 'What's wrong with *you*?' asked Wilmot, picking up Frank's quivering body.

'Frank saw B–B–Bearded Man! Wilmot fought B–Bearded Man.'

'Bearded Man?' repeated Lunetta as she joined them in the hayloft.

'Oh,' said Wilmot, remembering his first attacker had a beard. 'Yes, the Bearded Man…' Wilmot hesitated before saying, 'I – I killed him. Don't worry, Frank, he's gone.'

'Won't take Frank away and never give him back?'

'Err – no, you're fine now. There's no need to be scared.'

'Wilmot hero! Wilmot hero! Wilmot protect us from Bearded Man!' chanted the four muckers, jumping up and down.

'I'm not sure what you've done, mate, but it's certainly made you very popular with this lot,' said Timothy.

'Oh…it's nothing,' said Wilmot, forcing a smile. He hadn't realised the story he'd told Frank to keep him out of mischief at home had had such a lasting impact on him.

'Time to fill the marble I gave you, Wilmot,' said Lunetta. 'Just hold it tightly in your hand, fill your mind with every detail you can remember about your father's cellar and your imaginary thoughts will be preserved inside the marble forever.'

'What if it doesn't work?' said Wilmot.

'It's worth a try – isn't it?'

'Definitely,' he added, before a frown darkened his optimism. 'I *really* hope this works.' Squeezing the marble in his sweaty palm, Wilmot shut his eyes and let his enhanced imagination begin to work. He tried to remember every minor detail, from the distinctive smell of the cellar to each colourful vial on his father's experimental bench, as he pictured it in his mind. When he'd finished, he cautiously opened one eye and then the other. 'I've done it.'

'Let's see,' said Timothy.

Wilmot held the marble up to examine it. 'I can't see much...' He frowned. 'Half of it's too dark, and the other half has too many bright, glowing colours.'

'The marble looks very pretty,' said Eve, standing on tiptoes to take a look.

'The bright colours must be the colourful vials. But I'm not sure...' Wilmot took a deep breath.

'Frank goes with you. Wilmot not be alone.' He smiled one of his endearing all-teeth grins.

'We can't all go with you,' said Eve, 'there would be too many hands trying to hold one marble at the same time. I think Timothy should go to the cellar with Wilmot.'

'I agree,' said Lunetta. 'Best mates should stick together. We'll stay here and wait for you to return.'

'Come here, Johnny,' said Timothy, picking up his mucker.

'Ready, Timothy?' Timothy nodded. Wilmot took a deep breath and picked up Frank. 'I really hope this works.'

'Bye, girls, see you soon,' said Timothy, taking Wilmot's hand as the marble began to warm.

'Bye!' said Wilmot, hoping he'd see them both again soon.

A flash of blinding light appeared, and seconds later they both disappeared.

CHAPTER THIRTEEN

Wilmot landed in a dimly lit room. A square of diffused light, high above, provided minimal illumination.

'Are we in the cellar?' whispered Timothy.

Wilmot breathed in the familiar damp smell that reminded him of his father. 'I think so.' Broken glass crunched under his feet as he turned to look around. 'Although...I'm quite sure I didn't put the broken glass here. This is how the cellar looked after Frank destroyed it – I didn't imagine it like this.'

'Are you sure?' asked Timothy, bumping into an experimental bench littered with broken vials.

'Oh no! The marble's taken me to the real cellar – it's taken me back home! Or, maybe, the marble's just a figment of my imagination! It's all a *dream*! You're not really here either – are you?'

'Wilmot, calm down. I am here,' said Timothy, gently touching his arm.

Wilmot flinched. 'If I'm not dreaming, where are all the colourful vials I imagined in the marble?'

'Don't panic, Wilmot, remember your imaginary place could be made up of a mixture of different imaginations that have overlapped with your father's and anyone else's that might've visited him here.'

'Okay...I'm not dreaming,' he mumbled to himself. 'This is all real and I'm not...' Wilmot heard a shuffling noise and turned sharply. 'Was that you?'

'No,' whispered Timothy. 'Sounds like we're not alone.'

'Where's Johnny?'

'I've got him.'

'Where's Frank?'

'I've got him too,' said Wilmot. He heard the shuffling noise again. 'Hello. Is anyone there?'

No one replied.

'It's circling us.' Wilmot put Frank safely inside his pocket and reached for his sword. 'My sword – it's gone. I'm back in my coat and pyjamas again. Timothy, have you got your sword?'

'Did you imagine one for me?' Timothy felt around for a sword, but he was dressed in his black school jumper, white polo shirt and black trousers without any weapons.

'No.'

'Then, *no*, I haven't got one.'

Wilmot closed his eyes.

'It's too late to imagine a sword *now*. You're supposed to imagine the swords *before* we get here.'

'Oh, great, now what?'

Heavy breathing now accompanied the shuffling noise as the 'whatever it was' began to circle them, gradually pacing faster and faster like the thudding paws of an irritated tiger in a confined zoo enclosure assessing two very unwelcome guests, creating a whirl of choking dust.

'What are we going to do?' Wilmot coughed.

'Run!' shouted Timothy, pointing to a crack of light in the wall ahead.

Timothy grabbed Wilmot's arm as the 'whatever it was' jumped through the thick suspended dust, growling with bared teeth.

'AAAAAH!' Wilmot screamed, the creature's jaws snapping like nuts breaking in a nutcracker close behind him.

'Push!' cried Timothy, thumping the side of his body against the expanding crack in the wall and pounding it with his fist.

Wilmot's body jolted forward as two enormous paws flopped over his shoulders. The creature panted warm, damp air on his neck. 'HEEEEELP!' he cried, bashing his fists against the crack with Timothy.

The crack, which now appeared to be a strip of light between a set of closed doors, burst open.

'AAAAAH!' cried Wilmot.

With nothing but air to keep him upright, he fell forward, landing face down on the dusty floor beside Timothy. The creature bounded on top of him. His body pressed against the hard floor, bending his ribs like a sumo wrestler's bedsprings, as he writhed around trying to free himself from the beast. Stale-smelling saliva dripped on to his neck as the creature's jaws gripped and shook his coat hood, growling into his ear. His coat zip pressed into his throat, choking him. He turned his head to relieve the discomfort, knocking his chin against the hard, cold floor.

'Help!' said Wilmot in a muffled voice. Wet saliva trickled down his neck.

'WOOF! WOOF! WOOF!'

Wilmot heard hurried footsteps heading towards him.

'Timothy!' shouted Wilmot. 'Timothy, help me!' The creature continued mauling his coat, causing his face to scratch against the rough surface of the dusty floor.

A pair of tatty, brown leather shoes stopped at Wilmot's head. Almost instantly, the creature let go of his coat and sat upright, lumping its entire bodyweight on the base of his spine. Its humungous feet began to pad Wilmot's shoulders, squeezing any remaining air from his body like a punctured tyre on a bumpy road, as he fought to breathe.

'Good boy,' said a man with a strange voice. He spoke as if he were talking through his nose.

'He's lovely,' said Timothy. 'What's his name?'

'Barnes Wallis – or Wallis for short.'

'Can someone *please* help me!' protested Wilmot. The heavy creature licked the back of his exposed neck with its moist tongue.

'It's the name of the person who invented the bouncing bomb in the Second World War. It's the perfect name for him because he bounces into everyone and everything he touches,' continued the man. 'I'm Monty,' – holding out his hand – 'it's nice to meet you.'

'I'm Timothy,' he said, shaking Monty's hand. 'You'd better get your dog off my friend. He's not looking too happy under there.'

'Down, boy!' commanded Monty.

As the weight of the dog lifted away from Wilmot's body, he let out a long gratifying groan and rolled on to his side in case the dog tried to jump on him again.

'Are you all right, mate?' asked Timothy, tensing his lips to hold back a smile.

'Just great,' he muttered, looking up at the sad, droopy eyes of a huge St Bernard dog. The dog shook its body – spraying drool in every direction, as its chops smacked against its large teeth – until

142

its long brown and white fur had fluffed up like an electrified mohair jumper. 'What's *his* problem?' Wilmot lowered his arm, which had been shielding his face from the flying spit.

'I think he likes you,' said Timothy, smirking.

Wallis padded over to Wilmot and licked his face, leaving a diagonal strip of dust-free skin. 'Get off me, you slobbering mutt!' Wilmot shooed the dog away, got to his feet and wiped his sleeve across his face, covering himself in even more dust, before he was licked again. 'Likes me? Oh, that's why he tried to bust my ribcage, because he *likes* me?'

Frank jumped out of Wilmot's pocket and climbed up Wallis's leg, grabbing handfuls of hair, until he was sitting next to Johnny who had just settled into a comfortable position on the dog's back.

'I'm Monty. It's nice to meet you,' he said, offering a hand to Wilmot. 'Don't worry about Wallis – he's a gentle giant. I know it's hard to believe but, your friend's right, he seems to have taken an instant liking to you.'

Monty towered above Wilmot. He was bald on the top of his head– apart from a few strips of brushed-over greying hair – with shorter messy hair around the back and sides. He had a prominent nose with rather large hairy nostrils, dominating Wilmot's view of him from below. Over his thin, gangly body he wore a white laboratory coat, far too short in length, with sleeves that ended half way up his long skinny arms.

'It's nice to meet you too. My names Wilmot,' he said, shaking his hand. 'I was hoping to meet my father here. Do you know William Madder?'

Monty stared wide-eyed at Wilmot. 'Are you *Wilmot Madder* – William Madder's son?'

'Yes, I am.'

Monty turned sharply. 'Quickly! We've no time to waste. Follow me!'

CHAPTER FOURTEEN

Wilmot hurried through the room, squeezing past numerous experimental benches, following Monty. Wallis bounded ahead, carrying the two muckers on his back, knocking over everything his clumsy body was unfortunate enough to touch. An obvious explanation, thought Wilmot, for all the broken equipment he'd seen earlier.

'Where are we going? Do you know my father? Can you take me to him?'

'Ten years – an entire decade he's been waiting for this moment,' said Monty, 'now his ridiculous idea has jeopardized everything.' He sped up, his gangly legs exaggerating every footstep like an agitated spindly cartoon character.

'What and who are you talking about?'

'You'll find out soon enough. Keep up, boys!'

'Wow! Your cellar at home must be massive!' said Timothy. 'It seems to go on forever.'

'It isn't this big at home. Someone else must have imagined it like this.'

'Someone like your father – he must be here, Wilmot.'

'Woof! Woof!' Wallis became suddenly excited.

'We're nearly there!' said Monty, checking the boys were sticking close behind. 'Keep up!'

Wallis stopped and jumped excitedly on the spot. Wilmot tried to see past Monty's zigzagging body, but he blocked most of Wilmot's view.

'Wilmot's here!' said Monty, breathlessly. 'He's made it to Madder's World!'

'Is it your father?' asked Timothy.

'I don't know.' Wilmot ran on tiptoes to get a better view.

'Wilmot?' said a man, clearing his croaky voice. 'Wilmot's here?'

Wilmot slowed down. 'D – Dad?' He stared at the man standing almost close enough to touch. Was it his father? This man looked older than the father he remembered – older than the holographic image he'd seen in the cellar. His mad brown hair was beginning to grey, and his straight slender posture seemed more hunched...but his kind eyes were still...

146

'Wilmot,' said the man, 'you've changed...you look so grown-up.'

'Dad!' Wilmot rushed forward.

'You've made it! My son, you've actually made it to Madder's World!' said Dad, holding out his arms to embrace him.

Tears of joy trickled down Wilmot's cheeks. 'I can't believe it – I've found you!' He rushed forward into his father's arms, connecting like the lost piece of a puzzle.

'This is absolutely wonderful! Are Madeline and Nadine here too?' he asked, peering over Wilmot's head. Dad stepped back, holding both of Wilmot's hands, to take a good look at his son.

'No, it's only me.'

'*Only you* – it's magnificent – you've made it to Madder's World all on your own.' Dad squeezed his son's hands.

'Hello, Mr Madder,' said Timothy, holding his hand out to him.

'Timothy, it's good to see you again.' Dad shook Timothy's hand as Frank began to tug impatiently at his trousers. 'Frank, you're here! It's been a long time – too long!' added Dad. He leaned forward to pick him up but stumbled back clutching his chest.

'Dad, what's wrong with you?'

Mr Madder dropped down on a nearby stool. His whole body quivered, stopped momentarily and then quivered again in several short spasms as if he were receiving a series of acute electric shocks. As soon as his body settled, he leaned forward and patted Frank fondly on the head. 'I'm fine, don't worry–'

'He's *not* fine – that's why I brought you both here so quickly,' interrupted Monty. 'Wilmot, you've got to help us. Your father had this *crazy* idea. To jump start his heart, he gathered as many muckers as he could and told them all to bounce repeatedly at his chest.'

'Did it work?' asked Wilmot.

'Yes, it worked, but now his heart is beating too fast,' informed Monty, irritably. 'Your father has experimented with hundreds of different ways over the years to try to start his heart because he died and came to Madder's World before solving the problem. A beating heart is essential for everyone here because it would act like a clock to let us know when it's time to leave Madder's World. However, if your father's heart is beating too fast, his time here will tick away much too quickly!'

'Stay here. Don't leave Madder's World, Dad. Why would anyone want to leave such an amazing place anyway?'

'We all get older in Madder's World,' informed Monty. 'If we continue to grow old for all eternity it would be a fate worse than death itself. Nothing lasts forever. We must take the natural course and pass on to the next world to be with our loved-ones who die of old age and never come here. Only a beating heart will allow us to do this – it's the only way of knowing when our lives would've ended naturally if we had not died prematurely.'

Wilmot knelt next to his father. He opened the buttons of his laboratory coat to show Wilmot his heart hammering inside his ribcage, pulsing like an entangled fish in a net.

Monty continued to explain: 'Every individual is born with a heart that has a finite number of beats – when the heart stops, life ends. So, the faster it ticks, the sooner your father will leave us. He may only have a few months left, possibly weeks, if we don't slow it down.'

Wallis rubbed his large head against Dad's leg and whined as if he understood everything Monty had just said.

'I've just found you...I don't want to lose you again,' said Wilmot.

'I'm really sorry I died when you were so young, son.'

Wilmot hesitated. 'You had cancer, Dad...you don't need to apologise for something you had no control over.'

'No, but after the diagnosis, I did all I could to prepare myself for death. Luckily, I was given a rough idea of how long I had left to live, which gave me time to pick my own burial plot, complete Frank and create Madder's World, so that one day I'd see you again.' His body shuddered like a malfunctioning android, until the shaking gradually reduced to a slight twitch.

Wilmot held his father's hand while he waited for the trembling to stop. 'Are you...okay?'

Dad shook his arms and legs. 'It'll pass, my son, don't worry.'

'I can't believe you created all of this, so that I'd see you again.'

'And I did it for your mother and sister, of course. Unfortunately, I died before I'd solved the heart problem.' He paused, contorting his face to try to ease the numerous muscles twitching in his cheeks. 'Regretfully, I also died before I told your mother about Madder's World – I wanted to make sure everything was perfect before I took her with me. But, thankfully, I left the holographic message and Frank knowing he'd help you find your way when you were old enough if I died before it was all complete – your mother would have found the journey extremely difficult with two young children anyway.' He rubbed his hands against his cheeks to ease the twitching muscles.

'Well, it worked. And this place is amazing, Dad.' Wilmot smiled. 'Falling through your grave was a bit freaky though. Is it the only way to Madder's World?'

'No, not just my grave; the grounds of the entire graveyard and the adjoining crematorium access Madder's World,' informed Dad as the muscle twitching gradually increased down the left side of his face again. He slapped his cheek, triggering another short spasm, which rippled through his body all the way down to his trembling fingertips. Flexing each finger like a concert pianist preparing to play, he tried to alleviate the obvious discomfort. 'That's…a bit better.' The muscles in his contorted face slowly relaxed.

Wilmot waited for his father to recover fully before speaking. 'I'd do anything not to lose you again. Please, tell me how I can help?'

Monty frowned. 'Only the living can return to the real world. Are you still alive, Wilmot?'

'I – I think I am.'

'Have you been given a reflection box?'

'No, I haven't got one of my own.'

'Then we need to give you an unused marble,' said Monty. 'Churchill! Where are you? Lazy good-for-nothing mucker – he's always asleep when I need him,' he muttered. 'Churchill!'

Wallis joined in the search. It wasn't long before he came back with a ball between his teeth. He dropped it in front of Monty in a pool of dribble. Monty shook off the excess saliva and held the ball close to his mouth. '*Wake up*!'

Pop! Pop! Pop! Pop!

The mucker opened his sleepy eyes and gave a straight-postured soldier's salute. 'Yes, Sir!' he replied, followed by a wide yawn. He readjusted the army-green sock he was wearing so that it sat squarely on his head, resumed his rigid posture and waited for his next command.

'Reflection box,' said Monty.

'Yes, Sir,' replied Churchill with another salute. He retrieved the box from a nearby bench and rushed back to Monty.

Monty sifted through his marbles and found an unused one. He held the marble out to Wilmot. 'You must go back to the real world and find a scientist called Dr Allen.'

'Who's Dr Allen?' asked Wilmot, taking the marble.

'He's an old colleague of mine,' said Dad, looking quite dizzy after another series of short shudders. 'He has extensive knowledge of all the organs in the body and, most importantly, he specialises in matters concerning the heart.'

'Tell him we need his help,' added Monty. 'You must convince him to come back with you to Madder's World, so that he can help your father.'

'What if I can't convince him to come?'

'You'll do it, Wilmot,' said Timothy, 'I know you will.' Wilmot smiled back diffidently.

Monty continued: 'This time you need to ask Frank to hold the marble and fill it with his thoughts of the real world, so that he can transport you back home. The marble will disintegrate to nothing but dust as soon as you've reached your destination. It can never be used again.'

'Frank can get me home?' asked Wilmot. He grimaced at the grinning mucker sitting on his father's lap. 'Can I...trust him?'

'If you want to go back home, then you have no choice,' insisted Monty.

'Take this,' said Timothy, passing Wilmot the marble containing his father's cellar. 'I'll fill one of my empty marbles with the image of the cellar and come back with Lunetta and Eve to meet you here when you return.'

'Don't worry, Dad, I'll be back as soon as I can. I'll find and bring Dr Allen to Madder's World – even if I have to drag him all the way.' Wilmot placed the marble Timothy gave him safely inside his coat pocket and gave Monty's marble to Frank. 'Frank, fill the marble with the image of home.'

Frank took the marble and shut his eyes. 'Frank will think of Wilmot's house. Frank think of his favourite place in Wilmot's house.'

Wilmot gave Dad a hug and kissed his quivering cheek. 'I'll be back as soon as I can. See you soon, Timothy.' He patted Wallis's head and looked up at Monty. 'Please look after my Dad for me.'

'I'll not leave his side.'

'Good luck, son.' Dad smiled.

Frank took Wilmot's hand. The marble warmed between their palms.

Wilmot was on his way home.

CHAPTER FIFTEEN

Wilmot landed face down. His nose was pressed into a soft, fluffy pink surface, which looked surprisingly similar to the carpet in his sister's bedroom.

'Get out!' yelled Nadine, leaning over the side of her bed. 'Get out of *my room*, you *creep*!'

'What's going on up there!' called Mum from downstairs.

'Wilmot's been sleeping on my bedroom floor!' she exclaimed, flicking her long hair away from her face.

'Calm down – I'm leaving,' he said, scrambling to his feet. He scanned the pink room, looking for Frank, watched by the amused eyes of a hundred boys staring back at him from the boy band posters covering her walls.

'*Get out!*'

Narrowly missing a thrown pillow, Wilmot backed out of the door and headed for his own room. Nadine's alarm clock went off.

What time was it? What *day* was it?

'Breakfast's nearly ready!' called Mum. 'Get up! We don't want to be late for the convention!'

'Oh no…' Wilmot whispered to himself. How could he go to the convention now? He couldn't go without finding Frank.

Wilmot entered his room. There was no obvious sign that Frank was there either. He lifted his pillow and checked under his duvet. He knelt down to look under his bed. He looked in his wardrobe and his chest of drawers. He searched every possible hiding place, but Frank was nowhere to be seen.

'Breakfast's ready!' shouted Mum.

Wilmot came out of his room and stared at his sister's closed door. Was Frank in Nadine's room? He wouldn't be able to go in there now – she'd go mental if he attempted to step one foot in her room! He walked past, listening for any sound that might reveal Frank's whereabouts. Nothing. With no obvious sign of Frank's location, he hurried down the stairs. The quicker he ate his breakfast the more time he'd have to look for Frank upstairs when Nadine came down to eat.

'Wilmot!'

'I'm here, Mum.' He scanned the room. There was nothing to indicate Frank was here either.

'Oh, I didn't hear you come in,' she said, walking into the dining room carrying a frying pan. 'Are you...cold?'

'No,' he replied. He sat down at the table.

'I'm just wondering why you're wearing your coat over your pyjamas?'

He smiled sheepishly. 'Err – yes, I was a bit cold actually – when I first got up – but I'm fine now.' He started unzipping his coat but stopped halfway, his eyes fixed in a stare without focusing on anything, when he suddenly remembered his missing chest skin. He let go of the zip and discreetly slid his hand beneath his pyjama top and sighed with relief– his chest skin had returned. 'Thank...'

'What?' asked Mum, trying to slide her spatula under the fried egg spitting oil like a lighted sparkler in the frying pan.

158

'Oh, nothing,' he replied. His actual skin was obviously only visible back in the real world. He took off his coat and hung it on the back of his chair.

'You look shattered.' She placed the fried egg on top of the piece of toast already on his plate. 'Eat your breakfast. We've got a long day ahead of us. And wash your face. Honestly, you look like you've had your head stuck in a coal bucket.'

Wilmot tucked in. He'd wash the remaining dust off later.

'Slow down – you'll give yourself indigestion. Anyone would think you'd been out all night the way you're eating.' She headed back into the kitchen.

Wilmot scoffed down his food, eyes fixed on the door, waiting for Nadine to come down for her breakfast. He hoped she'd decide to eat now and tart herself up later. Nadine's bedroom door slammed shut. *Yes!* On hearing her footsteps on the stairs, he stuffed the last piece of toast into his mouth and gulped down the remainder of his fresh orange juice. Frank had to be hiding in her room.

'I'm going upstairs to have a wash,' he said, spitting bits of blended toast and juice over the table. He slid his chair back, almost knocking it over, and got up to leave the room.

'You'd better stay out of my room, *weirdo*!' said Nadine, passing him in the hallway. Her tall, slim frame towered over him. He kept his head down without saying a word. As soon as she was out of sight, he leaped up the stairs, two steps at a time, and headed straight for her room.

'We've run out of milk!' shouted Mum. 'I'm just nipping to the shop, Wilmot, is there anything you need while I'm there?'

'I'll go to the corner shop for you, Mum,' said Nadine. 'Just give me a second to change out of my pyjamas.'

Wilmot listened through the crack in Nadine's partially opened door. He'd just entered her room – he hadn't even started looking for Frank yet and Nadine was already coming back upstairs. 'No, Mum, I don't want anything!' he shouted back. *Please – please, don't come up to your room.*

'Thanks for offering, Nadine, but I want to choose a newspaper as well. I'll only be a few minutes,' replied Mum.

The door slammed shut. Wilmot let out the breath he'd been holding and waited for Nadine's footsteps on the stairs. After a few silent moments, and no sign of Nadine, he clicked the bedroom door shut and carried on searching her room.

Separating each hanging garment from the next, he sifted through Nadine's wardrobe. 'Frank, this isn't funny. *Where are you?*' he whispered. Several items slipped off their hangers and fell. He stuffed the clothes spilling out of her wardrobe back inside and closed the doors, jamming one garment as it slipped through the gap at the bottom before the doors were fully shut. 'Frank, I'm serious, come out *now.*' He knelt down to look under her bed, pushing Nadine's untidy school folders from one end to the other, but there was still no sign of him. Wilmot spun round and yanked at the stiff bottom drawer of her clothes chest. Nothing. He searched through three more drawers, checking between the layers of predominantly pink and purple clothing, before closing each one without success. 'Frank, *where are you*?' He stared at the top drawer, containing Nadine's underwear, and sighed. If Frank wasn't hiding in this drawer, the last one, Wilmot had no idea where to search next. He grimaced – the thought of going through his sister's underwear was not a pleasant one – opened the drawer and began to sift through. Seconds later, the bedroom door flew open.

'What are you *doing*?' yelled Nadine, charging forward to snatch her bra from Wilmot's grip.

'Nadine, I'm only...calm down,' he said, holding both hands out and backing off. Wilmot noticed Nadine's socks moving in the top drawer – Frank? 'Nadine, I can explain.' He stared at the gradually rising socks and then at Nadine's angry face. 'Please, Nadine, I need you to leave. I – I need you to get me something downstairs.'

'You're asking *me* to leave *my* room!' She glared at him as if one blink of her eyes would act as the detonator for the rage about to explode from her pursed lips.

Frank shook the socks from his head and climbed over them to the end of the drawer. Nadine, staring at Wilmot with bloodshot anger in her eyes, still didn't notice Frank who was now teetering on the edge of the drawer beside her, looking as if he might jump at any moment. Nadine's massive explosion was imminent!

Without time to explain, Wilmot lunged forward to grab him. But he was too late. Frank dived out of the drawer and, before he could stop him, sank his teeth into Nadine's bottom.

'AAAAAH!' Nadine screamed, rising to her tiptoes like a hot air balloon after a sudden blast of heat.

'Oh no,' said Wilmot.

'Something's biting my bum!' she cried, stamping her feet. 'Get it off!'

'I'm trying to help, but you need to stand still!'

'*Stand still*?' She grimaced. 'Just get it off me, *you idiot*!'

Wilmot gripped Frank's head and pulled.

'AAAAAH!' Tears rolled down her cheeks as she winced. 'You're making things *worse*!'

Wilmot pulled again, but Frank had a tight hold and was refusing to budge. 'I think I need to ask him,' said Wilmot. 'He only let go of me when I asked him.'

'I don't care how you get it off – *just do it!*'

'Please, let go, Frank!'

Frank released his grip and dropped to the floor as Mum opened the front door.

'I'm back!' she shouted, slamming the door behind her.

'Ooooh!' Nadine groaned. '*My bum is killing me!*' Nadine's jaw dropped as she turned and staggered back. '*What – is – that?*' she pointed at Frank, grinning up at her from the floor.

'Don't tell Mum. Please, Nadine, don't tell her – not yet.' Wilmot picked Frank up.

'Nadine, are you coming today?' asked Mum. 'Wilmot! Are you ready yet?' she shouted in frustration.

'Please, Nadine, Mum will freak out if she sees him in the house.'

Nadine backed towards her bedroom door with both hands covering her bum. 'I'll give you ten minutes, when I've finished my breakfast, to explain, if you make sure that that thing,' – gestures at Frank by nodding her head – 'doesn't bite me again.'

'Thanks, Nadine, I owe you one.'

'Owe me *one*! *Understatement* of the year!' Nadine slid through the gap in the partially opened door and closed it behind her.

'Thanks a lot, mate,' whispered Wilmot as soon as Nadine had gone. 'Why did you bring us to *her* room?'

'Wilmot's black and grey socks are boring. Frank like Nadine's brightly coloured socks.' He jumped out of Wilmot's hands, landed back in the top drawer and grabbed a handful of Nadine's socks.

'This isn't the first time you've stolen things from her room – is it? The sock you're wearing and the socks in the suitcase in the cellar are all hers too – aren't they?' Frank smiled mischievously. 'What are you doing?'

'Clothes for Johnny.'

'Don't even think about it.'

Frank's bottom lip protruded as he defied Wilmot and stuffed an odd red sock inside the one on his head. 'Just one odd sock,' he said, batting his eyes at Wilmot.

'You're *dead* if she finds out. And it's got nothing to do with me – right?' Frank nodded. Wilmot clicked the door open and peered through the crack. 'Quick – follow me.'

Back in his room, he racked his brain for a plausible explanation for Frank's existence. However, Wilmot couldn't think of anything – other than the truth – to explain a creature with a fat head that talked and had huge teeth for biting bums. He would have to tell Nadine everything. Could she cope with the possibility of losing her father again?

Nadine tapped lightly on Wilmot's door. 'Is it safe to come in?' she whispered, looking through a tiny crack in the door. 'Where is it?' Her eyes shifted from one corner of the room to the next.

'*He's* here,' said Wilmot, pointing to his lap. 'Have you said anything to Mum?'

'No, not yet, but you'd better have a good reason for me not to tell her.'

Wilmot decided he had no choice but to tell Nadine everything, from finding the cellar to meeting their father in Madder's World. He knew that if he didn't tell her, Frank was sure to tell her anyway.

Nadine stared at the wall, without blinking, listening to Wilmot reel off every detail of the last twenty-four hours. 'I don't believe it,' she said, holding her head in her hands. 'It can't be true. Dad's been dead for ten years.' She looked Wilmot directly in the eyes, raising both eyebrows. 'Very funny – this is all a big joke. You're winding me up…and *he's* nothing more than a mechanical toy you've bought to play a trick on me.'

'No, believe me, Frank's not a toy. Everything I've told you is true. We need to help Dad. We have to find a way to slow his heart down. If it continues to beat too fast, it'll reduce the time we have left with him and we'll lose him all over again. Let me prove it to you – help me find Dr

Allen, and then we can go to Madder's World together.'

'It all sounds mad, too unreal to be believable, but I can't help wanting it to be true. The thought of seeing Dad again...I'd love to go to Madder's World – if it is a real place.' Nadine sighed. '*If* it's true, and you are telling me the truth, we'll have to keep it a secret from Mum, because she couldn't cope with losing Dad twice. Here's the deal – I'll help you find Dr Allen if you promise to take me with you to Madder's World?'

'I will – as long as you promise *not* to tell *anyone* about anything I've told you.'

'Promise.'

'Nadine come with us!' said Frank, bouncing on Wilmot's lap.

'OMG – it can speak!' She stepped back. Her eyes narrowing as she stared at him with contempt. 'W*hat* is it wearing?'

'Oh, just some old sock.'

'It looks familiar. I'm sure I had some socks like that when I was younger. Has he been in my underwear drawer before?'

'Err…I'm not sure.'

'I hope you two aren't arguing up there?' shouted Mum.

'No, we're just talking!' Nadine shouted back. 'Keep *him* out of my room,' she whispered. 'I'll know if anything's gone missing.'

Suck! Suck! Suck! Suck!

Frank transformed into a ball before she took his precious sock away and found the other sock he'd just stolen from her room.

Nadine shuddered. 'I have absolutely no idea what that…*thing* just did, but promise me you'll keep a firm grip on it,' she insisted, 'especially near Mum.'

'Promise.'

'Hurry up! I'm ready and waiting to leave for the convention!' shouted Mum. 'Nadine, have you decided whether or not you're coming yet?'

'Yes! I'm coming – I'm coming!' she yelled back, closing Wilmot's bedroom door.

Wilmot had a quick wash, changed his clothes and put Frank safely inside his coat pocket before joining Mum and Nadine already waiting in the car.

He kept silent during the journey, staring distantly through the window, trying to absorb the enormity of the secret he was keeping from his mother.

Within an hour, they'd arrived at the *Grand City Hall*. It was an old building, inspired by Roman architecture, with a number of wide steps that decreased in size as you approached four huge marble pillars – two on each side of the massive oak door – standing like permanent guards.

Mum was greeted at the entrance and was eagerly whisked off by one of their father's old friends to update her on the day's events. Wilmot and Nadine both promised to meet her in the main conference room at one o'clock for their father's tribute speech.

'We should be helping Dad. This *stupid* convention is a complete waste of time!' Nadine groaned.

'Stop moaning. I feel just as frustrated as you.' A programme of the day's events was thrust in his face as they were ushered past the bustling entrance and into the main hall. 'Maybe there's someone here who knows where we can find Dr Allen.'

Nadine's eyes widened. 'Or, maybe, he's here already!'

Wilmot opened his programme, listing all the scientific exhibits on display, and ran his finger down them to look for any mention of Dr Allen.

Nadine peered over his shoulder. 'Number fifty-three,' – she pointed – 'Allen's Elixir!'

'Do you think it's him?' he asked. He turned and looked optimistically into her eyes.

Nadine checked her watch. 'We've got just under two and a half hours to find out.'

CHAPTER SIXTEEN

The *Grand City Hall's* main hall was huge. It had a vast ceiling with decorative plaster mouldings around its edge and circular mouldings at the base of several elaborate brass-light fittings that hung evenly spaced throughout the hall. The cream ceiling and walls, which were probably once white, bounced the echoes of chatter from the packed hall into a continuous hum like a buzzing beehive.

Wilmot moved with the slow-moving crowds, looking through the gaps between the bodies of the people surrounding him. 'I can't see anything.'

Nadine, who was taller, looked over some of the shorter people's heads. 'This is ridiculous. Exhibit four is next to exhibit thirty-one, and exhibit twelve is next to number fifty. None of them are in order!' She moaned.

'We've got to keep looking. I'm sure we'll come across exhibit fifty-three eventually.'

'This is an absolute nightmare. It's far too packed in here.' Nadine stopped behind a group huddled near an exhibit where a man was claiming he could cure severe migraines in ten minutes. 'I might need some of that headache stuff before the end of the day.'

Wilmot rolled his eyes. 'Concentrate, Nadine, exhibit fifty-three has to be here somewhere. Which direction shall we head in?'

'You choose – I'm sure it'll stink of horrible sweaty bodies whichever direction we head in.'

Wilmot pulled Nadine's arm and dragged her with him. 'Will you ever stop moaning? We'll go this way.'

Wilmot checked exhibit after exhibit until he finally ran out of exhibits. He stood at the far end of the hall and stared out at the crowds, moving like disorientated worker ants assessing the damage to their nest after a termite invasion, and sighed.

'I'm sure we've seen all of them now,' said Nadine. 'He's not here. He probably couldn't come – he might be ill or something. We'd better head back. We've got under an hour to get through this lot and across to the conference room to meet Mum.'

'Dr Allen's got to be here somewhere,' insisted Wilmot, yawning through his words – last night's lack of sleep was beginning to creep up on him.

'What was that?' asked Nadine. 'It sounded like someone being…*sick*?'

Wilmot heard a second splat of liquid hitting the floor. 'Where's that sound coming from?' he asked, following Nadine who was already heading towards a partially dismantled exhibit.

'It's coming from behind this lot.' She lifted a large cardboard sign out of the way to look behind the exhibit. 'Urgh!' said Nadine, stumbling back. She held her nose. 'Disgusting! He's fallen in his own puke!' Nadine used the sign to hide her face. 'Let's go – I'm not staying here another minute.'

'He stinks!' said Wilmot, cringing at the sight of the short fat man lying on the floor in a pool of vomit. 'We'll have to tell someone. We can't just leave him here like this.'

'Yes, we can. I'm not helping that drunken idiot!'

Wilmot gasped. 'Nadine, the sign you're holding – look at the sign!'

She turned the sign and read it out loud, 'Allen's Elixir.'

'It's him! Nadine, we've found him!'

'Oh no, that can't be him.' She exhaled and grimaced at the man lying on the floor. 'Please, tell me that's *not* him.'

Wilmot climbed over the exhibit, stepping over a mountain of previously bent cardboard, and tapped the man's shoulder. 'Hello. Are you Dr Allen?'

'Oooh.' The man groaned, lifting his head out of the runny, yellow vomit.

'Are you Dr Allen?' Wilmot repeated, pinching his nostrils together.

'Who – wants – to know?' asked the man, slurring his speech.

'My name is Wilmot Madder. I believe you knew my father?'

'Are you William Madder's son?' whispered the man, rising clumsily to his feet. Vomit trickled down one side of his face. Wilmot nodded. 'Any child of William's is a friend of mine!' he shouted. 'I am the famous Dr Allen!' He hiccupped. A woman sped up as she passed by, looking slightly unnerved by his drunken behaviour. 'You're just like all the rest!' Dr Allen shouted at her. 'You'll be sorry when I'm one hundred and fifty years of age and you're *dead*!' he continued shouting, waving his finger at the poor woman disappearing into a group of people who had turned to see why someone was yelling. 'And the rest of you,' he added, his voice suddenly quiet again. He fell to his knees, crashing into a stack of cardboard.

'Keep *him* down there,' Nadine told Wilmot, through gritted teeth. She turned to face the onlookers. 'He's fine – there's no need to be alarmed – I'm...dealing with him.' She climbed over the exhibit, picked up a large cardboard cut-out of some oversized test tubes and propped it up against a wobbly table to hide Dr Allen. 'What are we going to do with him? He's out of his head.' She gripped her nose. 'And he smells totally *repulsive*!'

Dr Allen began to shake his head rapidly up and down.

'What's he doing *now*?' asked Nadine. 'He's mental! Dad's asked you to find a *total nutcase*!'

'Dr Allen, are you all right?' asked Wilmot.

'Absolutely fine,' he whispered, looking slightly dizzy from all the head shaking. He clambered off the flattened cardboard, pulled off his tweed jacket and used it to wipe the sick from his face. 'It's lovely to meet you!' he shouted, throwing his jacket to the floor. 'I feel much better now!' He tilted his head one way and then the other, stretching his neck on both sides. 'Nothing like a good shake of the head to ease the side-effects!'

'You're not drunk anymore?' asked Wilmot.

'Drunk? I wasn't *drunk* – I never touch alcohol, boy! The sickness is just an unfortunate side-effect of my Allen's Elixir!' he shouted.

'If you're not drunk, *why* do you keep shouting and whispering?' snapped Nadine. 'Are you *mad*?'

'Just another one of the unfortunate side-effects,' he whispered, followed by a series of hiccups. 'I find it extremely difficult to control the volume of my voice. It'll all wear off in an hour – no need to worry,' he continued, getting louder. 'I take Allen's Elixir every day at twelve! I never miss a dose!'

'Why? What does it do?' asked Wilmot.

'Drinking it daily will prolong the life of all the organs in my body. I'm expecting to be the first person to live to at least one hundred and fifty,' he whispered, 'almost another hundred years of life left in me yet, boy.'

'That's wonderful!' said Wilmot.

'Tell that to all those who have no faith in me!' he shouted, stumbling forward. 'My Elixir's been tossed aside and disregarded just because it makes you a *little bit sick*! I lost all my funding too! Appalling!' He puffed out his chest, waving his hand dismissively. 'They'll be sorry when I'm alive and they're all *dead*!'

'Dr Allen, I need to ask you something important,' interrupted Wilmot.

'Well, speak to me, boy. What is it?'

'We need you to come with us to a special place.'

'I'm a very busy fellow,' he said, pulling down his waistcoat, 'I'm not sure I can make that sort of promise,' he whispered.

'Before I ask you, I need you to meet one of my father's inventions.' Wilmot slid his hand in his pocket and pulled out a small ball. 'It will help you

178

believe everything I'm about to tell you. Frank, wake up!'

Pop! Pop! Pop! Pop!

Frank stretched his little arms.

'Good grief! What is *that*?' asked Dr Allen, leaning forward and adjusting his round metal-framed spectacles to take a closer look.

'This is Frank,' replied Wilmot, keeping a firm grip on him.

Frank grinned his usual all-teeth smile.

'He's got *huge* teeth!' shouted Dr Allen.

'All the better to bite you with,' muttered Nadine. 'Do you have to keep *shouting*?'

In a moment of lapsed concentration, Frank wriggled through Wilmot's fingers.

'Oh no! Quick! Catch him!' yelled Wilmot.

Frank headed straight for Dr Allen.

'AAAAAH!' Dr Allen screamed. 'Get it off!' His voice reduced to an angry whisper. 'It's biting my bum.'

'Frank, let–'

'No,' said Nadine. She pulled Wilmot back to stop him from helping Dr Allen with a calculating smile.

Wilmot, realising why she'd stopped him, smiled back. 'I'll get him off *if* you promise to come with us to a place called Madder's World.'

Dr Allen winced. '*Just get him off me*! I promise – I'll go anywhere you ask!'

Nadine covered her ears. 'Why is he *so* loud. Call Frank off!'

'Frank, please, let go!'

Frank opened his jaws and fell to the floor with a plop.

Holding on to the edge of the small wobbly table for support, Dr Allen breathed deeply.

'So you'll come with us?' asked Wilmot, lifting Frank up to threaten him with another potential bite if he said no.

'Have I any choice in the matter?' Dr Allen stared at Frank's bared teeth.

'No,' replied Wilmot and Nadine simultaneously.

Frank licked his lips.

'Let me explain why we need you to come with us.'

'This had better be good, boy,' insisted Dr Allen, rubbing his bottom.

Wilmot began to explain why they needed his help, including as much detail about the last twenty-four hours as possible, and how important it was for him to join them in Madder's World. Intrigued, although he made it quite clear he was still unconvinced by the whole story, Dr Allen eventually agreed to meet them at the cemetery.

'See you at midnight,' said Wilmot.

'On the dot – I'm never late.'

'But we are,' said Nadine, checking her watch. 'We've got to meet Mum in fifteen minutes.'

After a quick goodbye, they left Dr Allen and headed back into the bustling crowd.

'It is all true – Madder's World does exist?' asked Nadine. 'You wouldn't make it all up – would you?'

'Of course not.'

'It's just, well, I'm finding it all very hard to believe.'

Wilmot smiled as he tucked Frank safely inside his pocket. 'In under twelve hours we'll both be on our way to Madder's World – *then* you'll believe me!'

CHAPTER SEVENTEEN

Wilmot and Nadine arrived late, missing the first five minutes of their father's tribute speech, and were quickly ushered next to their mother in two reserved seats at the front of the room. Wilmot sat through the rest of the speech, eyes half closed, struggling to stay awake in the stuffy room.

'That was really lovely,' said Mum, looking quite emotional at the end of the speech. 'I feel very proud of your father.'

'Dad is an amazing man,' added Wilmot, shuffling out of the room behind her.

'He *was*,' she corrected him. 'The synthetic skin he was working on would've helped so many people in need of skin grafts. Imagine damaging your skin in a fire or a serious road accident and having replacement skin. The reflection box was a wonderful idea too. The possibility of storing all your favourite memories in one little box – simply brilliant!'

Wilmot didn't say a word.

After lunch, they had to endure four boring lectures, held by their father's old friends, and another tour of the exhibits until Mum finally decided it was time to leave.

'I'm shattered,' she said, walking back to the car. 'It'll be an early night for me tonight.'

Wilmot gave Nadine a discreet thumbs-up – Mum would sleep soundly tonight.

It was quite late when they arrived home. Wilmot slumped next to Nadine on the living room sofa, completely bloated after the takeaway he'd eaten on the way home.

'Nadine, stop fidgeting. You're not behaving normal,' whispered Wilmot. 'Mum will get suspicious if she sees you acting odd. Do something to take your mind off things.' He leaned forward, picked up the remote control and turned on the television.

'I can't help it. My mind feels more alert. My imagination's more active than usual,' she said, picking up the newspaper that Mum had left on the coffee table earlier. 'Wilmot, look at the headline! *Fugitive Fuller's Final Flee!*'

'They've caught him?'

'It looks like it. It says here that Timothy Sparks' killer died at the wheel.'

'He's dead?' Wilmot pressed the off button on the television remote before it fell from his slackened grip on to the table.

'Yes, it says that he crashed a stolen car during a police car chase and killed himself.' Nadine gasped as she followed the text with her finger. *'A post-mortem examination confirmed that he was more than five times over the legal drink-drive limit.* Serves him right!'

Wilmot stared at the front-page picture of the mangled car. 'I suppose it does,' he added, sad at yet another death even though it was David Fuller who was the casualty this time.

'Goodnight, Wilmot! Goodnight, Nadine! I'm off to bed!' shouted Mum from upstairs.

'Night, Mum!' they both shouted back.

Nadine looked at her watch. 'Shall we go to the cemetery now?'

'We can't go *now*. We told Dr Allen we'd meet him at midnight. It's too early,' whispered Wilmot.

He covered the opening of his moving pocket and spoke to Frank wriggling inside, 'Stay still. You can't come out.'

'What time shall we leave?'

'Eleven o'clock should give us plenty of time to get there.'

Frank continued to squirm inside Wilmot's pocket.

BURRRRRP!

A warm, wet patch dampened Wilmot's pocket, gradually increasing in size as it spread to his groin, making his trousers cling uncomfortably to his skin.

'Urgh!' Wilmot grimaced.

'Wilmot!' exclaimed Nadine, standing up and moving away.

'Oh no! He's done it again!' Wilmot stood up, pulling the wet fabric away from his skin.

'What has he done? You look like you've wet yourself.'

Wilmot yanked Frank, who was already changing from patchy blue back to his usual pale yellow colour, from his pocket. Globules of expelled fusion spray dripped on to the carpet. 'Thanks a lot, Frank!'

'He's relieved himself all over you.' She laughed.

'Are you two all right down there!' shouted Mum.

'Yes, Mum!' Wilmot answered, stuffing Frank back inside his sodden pocket.

'Keep the noise down! I'm trying to get to sleep!'

Wilmot waited for Mum's slippers to flip-flop along the upstairs landing and back across her bedroom floor before he spoke, 'I'd better clean this lot up and have a wash myself. Thanks, Frank, I'm completely shattered, and the last thing I need right now is to clean up after you.'

'I'll come and get you at eleven – no later,' said Nadine.

After he'd cleaned up and had a quick wash, Wilmot changed into some jeans and a thick blue sweatshirt ready for the journey. Frank refused to be cleaned. He preferred to remain covered in sticky, expelled fusion spray. Without the energy to argue, Wilmot tucked him under his pillow and got into bed. He desperately needed some sleep.

It seemed as if only minutes had passed, when he heard a light knock on his bedroom door and Nadine crept in wearing a purple tracksuit. 'Wilmot,' she whispered, rocking his body to wake him even though his eyes were already half open. 'Wake up.'

Feeling worse than he'd felt before, Wilmot sat up, rubbed his eyes and woke Frank. Without disturbing Mum, who was snoring loud enough to mask any noise they'd ever make, all three of them left the house.

Once outside, the fresh night air and spitting rain helped clear Wilmot's sleepy head. Quite sure Nadine would be unable to keep up if he ran too fast, he walked briskly through the drizzle. With each step the rain got heavier. By the time they reached the graveyard, it was pouring down.

Wilmot walked through the church gate – followed by Nadine who was walking so close she kept knocking the ends of her trainers into the backs of Wilmot's – and headed out into the graveyard.

'Where's Dr Allen? Can you see him?' asked Wilmot, holding his coat hood to stop the driving rain forcing it back against his face.

'I can't see anything in this rain. He'd better turn up, or– '

'Look!' Wilmot ducked behind a tall rectangular gravestone. 'Over there!' he said, peering over the gravestone and pointing at a dark figure.

The figure, wearing something that resembled a long cape, staggered towards them. The garment lifted with the turbulent breeze, flapping wildly like the wings of an enormous bat, before dropping back down.

'Be careful, Nadine, we don't know if it's him.' Almost ripping her arm from its socket, he pulled her down beside him. 'Stay here and wait until I can see who it is.' Wilmot watched the dark figure carefully as it moved closer.

'Is it Dr Allen?'

Wilmot pulled his head back down. 'I don't know.'

'Take another quick look,' insisted Nadine, repositioning her coat between her crouching body and thighs to keep it out of the wet mud.

The creepy figure lurched forward and began to retch.

'That's him – I'd bet money on it,' said Nadine, standing up. 'Nothing like projectile vomit to give your identity away.'

Wilmot zigzagged through the wet grass, avoiding the graves, to help him. 'Dr Allen, are you all right?'

'Hello, Wilm...' whispered Dr Allen, before vomiting again.

'He's totally *intoxicated*! How are we supposed to take *him* to Madder's World like *that!*' said Nadine. 'I thought he only took that stuff at midday.'

'I said I take it at twelve,' corrected Dr Allen, slurring his speech. 'It's twelve o'clock twice a day!' he shouted.

'It's *only* eleven thirty,' snapped Nadine, through gritted teeth.

'Close enough,' he added, hiccupping. He leaned against Wilmot and proceeded to button up his shiny black raincoat, placing the first button in the third buttonhole, until he finally reached the last buttonhole. 'All ready,' he whispered, trying to pull the uneven raincoat down on the shorter side.

Wilmot took Dr Allen's arm and led him, staggering at his side, in the direction of his father's grave, the rain beating against their stooped backs like falling shingle. Several times along the way, Dr Allen shook his head, so that by the time they'd trudged through the wet grass and reached the grave he seemed more in control of his unsteady feet.

Wilmot pulled Frank from his pocket and dangled him in the full force of the rain. 'That'll clean you up.'

'Frank not like it!' he protested, waving his arms and legs.

'Will he bite me again?' asked Dr Allen, instinctively sliding his hands over his bum to protect it.

'No, I don't think so. He only seems to bite when he meets someone for the first time.'

'Good, because my mind has been overactive ever since he bit me. My imagination's been so vivid that it's been driving me mad!' Dr Allen shouted, uncontrollably.

'My imagination has been the same,' said Nadine. 'In fact, now you mention it, it's been like that ever since Frank bit my bottom too.'

'Of course, it must be the fusion spray that Frank eats!' suggested Wilmot. 'Fusion spray enhances your imagination. Some of it must have transferred from his body to yours when he bit you.' Frank smiled his usual all-teeth grin. 'Is that why you bite people when you first meet them, Frank?'

Frank nodded. 'Nadine and Dr Allen need good imagination to travel to Madder's World.'

'I knew there had to be a reason for the bum biting. Without an enhanced imagination we'd never make it to the tunnel. A good imagination is essential for you to think of a safe mode of transport,' informed Wilmot, stepping on to his father's waterlogged grave. 'Close your eyes and use your enhanced imagination to help you think of a preferred way to travel. It's how I ended up in the car I told you about: I just pictured it in my mind and the next thing I knew I was driving it. Then, as soon as we reach the tunnel, we can pass through the circle of light together.'

'I'm scared, Wilmot,' said Nadine, rain trickling down her face like a torrent of tears.

'If anything goes wrong, just pass through the circle of light – focusing all your thoughts on the description I gave of the Waiting Room – and I'll meet you there.' He gestured for them to step forward. 'We've no time to waste – let's go.' They both joined Wilmot and stood on the grave. 'Six feet under!' said Wilmot, eager to proceed before they changed their minds.

From the safety of Wilmot's coat pocket, Frank began to chant his little rhyme. The ground shifted beneath their feet. Wilmot remained calm as his feet became trapped in the mud. Nadine and Dr Allen instinctively began to panic. Wilmot watched them both struggling to pull their feet from the mud. Nadine lost her balance, toppled and fell against Dr Allen, sending his arms flailing, flicking an unwelcome spray of rainwater into Wilmot's face.

As uncomfortable as they looked, Wilmot knew there was no other way to get to Madder's World. He wiped the water from his face and waited for the inevitable.

Frank repeated the rhyme to prepare them for the journey ahead, until the earth finally collapsed beneath all four of them.

Listening to their deafening screams, Wilmot plummeted to the depths below.

CHAPTER EIGHTEEN

Nadine's piercing cries echoed through the darkness as Wilmot descended, tumbling over and over, until he finally landed with a bump on a soft leather seat: he was back in the Aston Martin DB5. There was nothing he could do for Nadine or Dr Allen now.

Zipping Frank safely inside his coat, Wilmot put on his seatbelt and waited for the countdown to begin. Moments later, the car pulled back and catapulted off at awesome speed. Left once again to grapple in vain with the uncontrollable steering wheel, he watched the needle on the speedometer steadily rise until it reached the 'speed of dark'. Black spots danced before his eyes as he slipped in and out of consciousness. Finally, the spots merged to form one black mass.

The car jolted to a sudden stop. Wilmot opened his eyes in a daze, shook his dizzy head, undid his seatbelt and staggered out of the car, leaving the headlights on full beam, to check both ends of the tunnel for Nadine and Dr Allen.

There was no sign of either of them.

Wilmot heard a distant rumble. He turned to check the dark side of the tunnel again. Tiny vibrations passed through his feet and up his body. It had to be them. He squinted to see who or what it was.

A horse? The approaching silhouette continued charging towards him. Closer still. It was a horse. And Nadine was the rider.

'Stop!' shouted Wilmot, waving frantically.

'Wilmot!' cried Nadine, slipping sideways as she waved. 'HEEEEELP!'

'Slow down!'

Nadine quickly pulled herself back up.

Thundering behind her were at least another four horses, pulling a stagecoach, which Dr Allen appeared to be driving. He bumped against alternate ends of the seat, positioned at the front of the coach, sliding from left to right and back again, gripping the horses' reins with outstretched arms.

'Stop!' cried Wilmot, standing in the middle of the tunnel. 'Slow Down!'

Nadine continued to charge forward. 'I can't stop! I've never ridden a horse befooooore!'

Wilmot jumped out of the way, guarding his eyes from the clumps of mud flicking off the horse's hooves as it galloped past at tremendous speed. Seconds later, the horse swerved left to miss the car, throwing Nadine off balance again.

'Wilmot! Help meeeee!' she shouted. Nadine bumped repeatedly against the horse's flank, gripping the reins to pull herself upright.

Wilmot looked back at Dr Allen. It was clear to see that he had even less control of his stagecoach as it continued to career through the tunnel, narrowly missing the sidewalls. He had to stop Dr Allen and Nadine before they reached the circle of light. Neither of them seemed to be in control of their horses – he doubted whether they'd ever reach Madder's World in one piece if he didn't stop them now!

With no time to spare, Wilmot positioned himself against the tunnel wall, knees bent and arms extended, and waited for his moment to jump.

As soon as the stagecoach was close enough, Wilmot lunged forward and grasped the reins of one of the front-runners. His legs dangled a few centimetres from the ground. Quickly, he lifted them up and hung on tight.

'Hold on!' shouted Dr Allen, swerving to miss Wilmot's car.

Thumping against the animal's muscular torso, Wilmot attempted to pull himself up. With one foot pressed into the animal's ribcage, he pushed up and swung his leg over the horse's back to straddle its wide girth. Saliva frothed from the horse's mouth as it continued galloping forward, seemingly oblivious to Wilmot.

Wilmot twisted a handful of mane round his fingers, leaned forward and rested his head against the animal's sweaty neck. He could see Nadine's horse galloping in front of them. If she rode through the circle of light, without thinking of the

Waiting Room, there was a chance he might never find her in Madder's World.

'Faster!' yelled Wilmot.

'I can't go any faster!' shouted Dr Allen.

The gap between Wilmot and the circle was closing. Nadine's horse galloped closer and closer to the circle ahead of him.

'Heeeeelp!' she shouted. Seconds later, her horse jumped and disappeared into the circle of light.

'Remember the Waiting Room, Nadine!' cried Wilmot. 'Follow her, Dr Allen!' He closed his eyes and filled his mind with the image of the Waiting Room.

All four horses leaped forward, pulling the stagecoach with them.

'Hold on!' cried Wilmot as they passed through the circle of light.

Almost immediately, the stagecoach – along with all four of its horses – disappeared, and Wilmot was back in the Waiting Room with hundreds of mucker balls flying through the air. He ducked to avoid one hurtling straight at him, but it hit the side of his head and knocked him over. Lying on his back, he opened his coat pocket to check if Frank was okay.

Suck! Suck! Suck! Suck!

Frank instantly transformed into a ball and rolled off to join the others. Wilmot could see the balls were, once again, forming an impenetrable wall in front of another skeleton that was soon to be discarded from Madder's World.

'Help me!' cried the skeleton. He held his arms out to Wilmot as the rest of the people looked on from the far side of the room. 'Please! Help me!'

Wilmot scrambled to his feet and ran forward. 'Who are you?'

The lone skeleton backed away as the wall continued to push him. 'I need to say sorry! Will you find him and let him know I'm sorry?' cried the trembling skeleton, bobbing to look through the gaps between the mucker balls.

'Find who?' asked Wilmot.

'Timothy! Timothy Sparks!'

'David Fuller,' mumbled Wilmot, scarcely moving his lips. He froze, watching the desperate skeleton moving further and further away from him. Could he really help this man? He scurried forward. 'Are you…David Fuller?'

'I'm sorry – I didn't mean to kill him! I shouldn't have driven the car. I'd been drinking and… Please – please, tell them to stop! I need to find Timothy to let him know how sorry…' His bloodshot eyes darted from left to right, looking for an escape route.

Wilmot knew he only had a few moments left to help him before the back of the room opened. He flung himself at the wall of muckers but bounced back off and landed on the hard floor. 'Leave him alone!' he cried, scrambling to his feet.

'I should never have driven the car when I was… drunk.' The skeleton dropped to his knees, hunching into a protective ball, swaying as if on the deck of a ship battling a stormy sea. Peering between his forearms he cried, 'Please, can you find Timothy Sparks?' He wailed, momentarily, with panic-stricken terror. 'Please, find him for me?' The wall opened. 'Tell Timothy I'm so…'

Without uttering another word, the skeleton was sucked out into the dark void and left to slowly drift into oblivion. Wilmot watched helplessly as David Fuller's outstretched skeletal body floated peacefully away like a fading four-pointed star. When he was nothing more than a dull dot in the distance, the wall lifted to shut him out of Madder's World forever.

The hum of transforming mucker balls filled the room as everyone began to branch out and restore the room to its usual bustling self. There was nothing Wilmot could do to help him now.

'Wilmot!' shouted an angry voice.

Wilmot turned and looked up at an angry skeleton glaring down at him.

'What's happened to me?' said the skeleton.

'Nadine?'

'Where's my *skin*?'

'Nadine, let me explain.' He raised his hands and backed off.

'You never said anything about *losing my skin*!'

Another skeleton sauntered towards him. 'I've been trying to calm her down. But I think I might've made her worse.'

'Dr Allen?' asked Wilmot.

'I don't think it's *that* bad. How many people get the chance to look at their own skeleton – an unbelievable opportunity to marvel at their own anatomy,' continued Dr Allen.

Nadine turned sharply. 'Just shut up, you raving lunatic. How can having no skin be a *good* thing! You're completely *mental*!'

'It'll be fine,' insisted Wilmot. 'You'll get new–'

'Easy for you to say – you've got *your* skin!'

'I had to get synthetic skin when I first came here. It's the same for everyone on arrival.'

'If you think I'm seeing my father like this...' She sighed. 'You failed to remember to tell me my skin would *fall off,* and you also failed to tell me there'd be thousands of biting muckers here too. Is there anything else you've forgotten to tell me?' She placed her hands on her hips and waited for his reply.

'No – I – I don't think so.'

'Wilmot!' called a boy, pushing through the crowds of people.

'Timothy! Nadine, its Timothy!'

'Oh great – another person with skin – that makes me feel *so* much better.'

'It's good to have you back!' said Timothy.

'How's Dad?' asked Wilmot.

'There's been no improvement. But now you're here–'

'Hello, I'm Dr Allen.'

Timothy shook his skeletal hand. 'Wilmot persuaded you to come to Madder's World then.'

'With a little bit of help from Frank,' admitted Wilmot. 'Where is Frank?'

Two heads popped out of Timothy's trouser pockets. Johnny was already wearing the red sock on his head that Frank had stolen from Nadine's underwear drawer.

'Johnny found him.' Timothy pulled Frank out of his pocket and passed him to Wilmot.

'Did you hear David Fuller's apology?' asked Wilmot, taking Frank.

'Apology accepted. I'm happy here with my sister. At least he'll never be able to drive his car into anyone else now that he's dead too.'

'I think he paid the ultimate price,' said Wilmot, looking back at the closed wall.

'Hello, Nadine, you look a bit skinnier than I remember,' said Timothy with a wry grin. Wide-eyed, Wilmot shook his head as Nadine charged forward and framed up to Timothy. 'Only joking!' Timothy backed away from her, holding his hands up submissively. 'Where's your sense of humour.'

'It disappeared with *my skin*. What's this?' she asked, grasping unsuccessfully for the sock on Johnny's head. 'That's one of *my* socks!'

Frank grinned.

'I hope these socks aren't all mine?' she said, looking from mucker to mucker and then suspiciously back at Frank. Nadine pulled back her skeletal hand and stared at it in despair. As she moved the small bones of her fingers like the components of an unfamiliar machine, she caught a shocking glimpse of her blurred reflection in the shiny white floor and turned away. 'How can I see Dad for the first time in ten years looking like this?' She sighed. 'I've got to get some synthetic skin first.' Her eyes glazed over.

Wilmot rummaged in his coat pocket and took out a marble. 'Take this,' he said, handing her the marble, containing the image of Dad's cellar, he'd been given on his last visit. 'It doesn't take long to get new skin. Just join the people waiting for their skin over there,' – he pointed to a short queue – 'and as soon as you're done, you can meet me in the cellar using the marble like I told you – remember?' Nadine nodded.

Dr Allen handed Wilmot a small bottle of his Elixir. 'It's my midday supply. Give your father a few drops before I arrive. I'll go with Nadine to get new skin, and we'll meet you in your father's cellar as soon as we're done.' He headed off to join the back of the queue. 'See you in five,' he said, waving.

Nadine followed Dr Allen. 'Tell Dad I won't be long!'

Timothy retrieved his own marble that he'd filled with the image of the cellar in Wilmot's absence. 'Ready?' he asked, offering his hand.

Wilmot, feeling reluctant to leave without them, turned to check on Nadine and Dr Allen one last time before taking Timothy's hand. 'Let's go.'

The marble warmed between their palms.

Seconds later, they both disappeared.

CHAPTER NINETEEN

Wilmot's eyes gradually adjusted to the dim light. He was back in his father's cellar. 'Frank, are you okay?'

'Frank fine,' he replied, followed by an all-teeth grin.

'Timothy!'

'Over – here!' he cried, gasping for air between each word.

Wilmot moved between the benches and experimental clutter in the direction of Timothy's groans. 'Where? I can't find...' Before he'd finished his sentence, he found Timothy pinned to the floor, trapped beneath Wallis, drool dripping on to his face. 'He obviously likes you too,' said Wilmot, grinning. 'Down, Wallis!' As soon as Wallis jumped off, he helped Timothy to his feet.

While Timothy rearranged his clothes, Frank and Johnny climbed up to join their mucker friends (Lily, Gemmy and Churchill) already sitting on Wallis's fluffy back. The second they were in position, Wallis bounced off like an enormous rabbit to the end of the room where Wilmot found his father lying on a cleared bench. Monty, Lunetta and Eve were all watching over him.

'Dad, I'm back!'

'Wilmot, it's lovely to see you,' he said, turning his head wearily. Wallis jumped up and licked his face.

'Get down!' ordered Monty. 'Hello, Wilmot, Timothy. Did you find Dr Allen?' Wallis lumped his bottom beside Monty, his tongue hanging out of his mouth like a floppy, pink pork chop as he panted rhythmically.

Wilmot held his father's hand. 'Yes, he'll be here soon. I've brought Nadine with me too. They're both getting their new skin.'

Dad squeezed his hand and smiled. 'Thanks, son.'

Dad's heart was still pounding erratically in his chest while his whole body trembled in short irregular bursts. It was even more obvious now than when he'd left that Dad's condition was deteriorating. When he'd first held out his hand to greet Wilmot, his arm appeared thinner and weaker, his face notably pale and gaunt compared with the last time he'd seen him. Dad looked worse than he'd expected in such a short space of time.

'How are you feeling, Dad?'

'I've been better, son.'

'We've been looking after him since you left to get help,' said Lunetta.

Eve lowered her head. 'But I don't think we've been able to make him any better.'

Wilmot pulled the bottle of Elixir from his pocket. 'Dr Allen said this might help your heart.'

'What is it?' asked Monty.

'It's called Allen's Elixir – it's supposed to extend the life of all the organs in your body,' informed Wilmot, trying to get the bung out of the end. He twisted it unsuccessfully one way and then the other. 'Stupid bung.'

'Frank helps Wilmot.' Frank jumped up, gripped the rubber bung between his teeth and pulled. The bung flew out, with Frank still attached, propelling him through the air until he landed with a thump on the other side of the room.

'I'll get him,' said Timothy, rolling his eyes. He found Frank, picked up his limp body and shook it lightly. 'Oh no, Wilmot, I think he's knocked himself out!'

Concerned more about his father's health and less about another of Frank's antics, Wilmot pressed the small bottle of liquid to his father's trembling lips, ignoring Frank. A tiny drop of Elixir trickled into his mouth. 'Nothing's happening,' said Wilmot.

'Give him some more,' urged Monty, nibbling his fingernails.

Wilmot tilted the bottle until half of its contents dribbled into his father's mouth.

'Oh no!' cried Monty. 'Stop! Don't give him anymore! His heart is beating even faster!' He smacked both hands firmly against his cheeks, shaking his head from left to right in utter despair.

'What have I done?' said Wilmot, removing the bottle from his father's lips.

Suddenly, Dad's body began to shake in wild uncoordinated jerks. Then, wrinkles began to appear, like roads on a map, gradually widening and deepening across his face. Grey hair grew like thin strands of wire all over his head, and fine needles of brown and grey facial hair began to sprout from his face. His father's life seemed to be ebbing away. Like a dying flower observed through time-lapse photography, he was ageing at an alarming rate.

'He's ageing too quickly!' exclaimed Monty. 'If this continues, he could double in age within hours! We have to stop it!'

'Wilmot!' called Dr Allen.

'Where are you, Wilmot?' shouted Nadine.

'I'm over here! Dr Allen! Come quickly! We need your help!'

'Woof! Woof!' barked Wallis, hearing the strangers enter the cellar. Wallis bounded forward, knocking into Wilmot's legs. 'Woof! Woof!'

Wilmot stumbled sideways before regaining his balance. But it was too late: the bottle was empty and the remaining Elixir had spilt all over his father. Almost instantly, Dad's body stopped moving. Wilmot pressed the small bottle against his father's ribs in a fruitless attempt to catch the remaining drops dripping on to his father's already saturated heart.

A sudden hiss and Dad's ribcage filled with a red mist.

'Oh no!' exclaimed Wilmot, stepping back.

Blowing short puffs of air, Timothy tried to clear the red mist as it seeped into the room like gaseous blood. 'What's happening?'

'I don't know?' replied Wilmot, waving his arms to disperse the mist. 'How can we stop it?'

Monty grasped the front of his laboratory coat as if he might rip out his own heart and swap it for Mr Madder's faulty one. 'I don't know. I just don't know,' he replied.

'I'm sorry, Dad. I'm *so* sorry,' said Wilmot, taking his father's hand through the thinning red mist. Wilmot felt a light tremble pass through his father's fingers. With every passing moment, the trembling intensified until his father was shaking all over again. 'Dad, what's happening?' Wilmot held his father's hand until he was no longer able to stand close: Dad began to convulse, thrashing violently back and forth, limbs flailing, on the bench. 'Dad!'

Seconds later, he slipped off the bench and fell to the floor. Then, as quickly as they had begun, the convulsions stopped. Dad lay motionless on his back.

Wilmot flung himself to the floor beside his father's body. 'Don't leave me, Dad. Please…don't leave me.' Tears trickled down his cheeks. 'I can't…I can't lose you again,' he whispered, taking hold of his father's limp hand.

Eve knelt beside Wilmot. 'Wake up! Please, wake up, Mr Madder,' she pleaded.

'Mr Madder,' said Lunetta, her voice quivering as she tried without success to hold back her tears.

A sudden chill fell over Wilmot like an icy sheet covering his body, numbing his senses. Wrapping his arms around his father's torso, he pulled him close, letting out an uncontrollable sob. 'Don't leave me,' he whispered. Rocking his father's body, he wept against his lab coat – the normally reassuring damp smell did little to comfort him.

At least a minute or two passed, before a soft voice whispered, 'I'm not going anywhere, Wilmot.'

'Dad?' Wilmot released his tight grip and cradled Dad in his arms. 'But–'

'I'm okay, Wilmot. In fact, I don't think I've ever felt better,' he said, pulling himself up and rolling back his shoulders to straighten his posture. 'I have no idea what you gave me, but I don't think I've felt this good in years.' He looked down at his chest.

'Look at your heart!' said Monty. 'It's no longer beating rapidly! Your heart has slowed to a steady, regular beat! I don't believe it! Wilmot, you did it!' He rejoiced by clasping his hands together as if in prayer and dancing a funny little jig.

'It must have been when I dropped the Elixir,' said Wilmot, wiping away his tears. He turned to look for Dr Allen and Nadine. 'Dr Allen, your Elixir works! The Elixir cured Dad's heart problem when I dropped it directly on his heart.' He sniffed to clear his tear-congested nose.

'I'd love to – come – over – but–' said Dr Allen.

'There's a *massive, smelly, slobbery dog* on top of us!' interrupted Nadine. 'I can't...*breathe.*'

'Come here, Wallis!' called Monty. 'Get off those people – at once!'

Wallis lifted his large body off Dr Allen's legs and Nadine's chest before bounding across the room and rolling over submissively at Monty's feet – Dr Allen and Nadine both following close behind.

'Dad?' said Nadine, stopping to stare at the bearded man before her.

'Nadine! It's – it's so wonderful to see you.'

'I can't believe it! It is you! Dad, it's really you!' she said, rushing forward to embrace him.

'My Elixir worked?' asked Dr Allen.

'Yes, my old friend,' replied Dad, giving his daughter a tight affectionate squeeze. 'I'm glad you could make it.' He offered his hand.

'William, it's good to see you. I never thought I'd be seeing *you* again so soon though,' said Dr Allen, shaking his hand vigorously. 'I'm planning to live for at least another one hundred years. However, I might have to stop taking my Elixir orally from now on. It's obviously more effective when poured directly on to the organ,' he added, deep in thought.

'It's brilliant!' said Dad. 'Have you brought any more of it with you?' He smiled down at Nadine's glowing face staring up at him and strengthened his hug.

'I always carry a spare.' Dr Allen reached into his pocket and pulled out another bottle of Elixir. 'Have you any other problems that need rectifying? I'd love to try out the rest of my concoctions,' he added, opening his coat to reveal a row of small bottles attached to the inside lining. 'I've been working on several different combinations of my Elixir. It would have been nice to try out all of them. This one here,' – pulling out another bottle – 'is great for the brain. And I've also found it's quite good for new hair growth.'

Nadine turned to face Dr Allen. 'Well, he certainly doesn't need that right now,' she remarked, 'look at the length of his beard.'

Dad rubbed his hand over his new facial hair.

Monty took the bottle of Allen's Elixir. 'This one is exactly what we need. It's just what the doctor ordered.'

Wilmot frowned. 'One tiny bottle will never be enough to fix all the hearts in Madder's World.'

'One bottle is all we need,' said Dad. 'Now all we have to do is copy the formula and fill a marble with a place containing an endless supply.'

A groan came from a dizzy looking Frank in Timothy's hand. 'Wilmot! Frank's all right. He's waking up!'

Frank stretched his arms above his head and half opened his watery eyes before gazing across the room. Suddenly, his eyes opened wide – bulging out of their sockets as if a table tennis bat had just whacked the back of his head to reveal two hidden ping-pong balls. 'Wilmot!' he cried, dropping his arms and trembling from head to foot. 'Save Frank from Bearded Man!' he exclaimed, pointing at Dad.

Before Wilmot had time to explain, Frank launched his rigid body into the air. Seconds later, he smacked into Wilmot's head, hitting him directly between the eyes. Wilmot's eyes flooded with tears, rolling in circles like floating beach balls in their watery sockets, as Frank fell to the floor.

Staggering on the spot, Wilmot reached out, his hands grabbing at thin air, trying to grip on to anything that might prevent him from falling. Blinking rapidly, he tried to erase the black spots swimming in his blurred vision. But the more he blinked, the larger the merging blotches of ink grew.

'Quick! Help him. He's going to fall!' exclaimed Nadine.

A rush of hands grabbed Wilmot's body as he fell back. His head smacked against something hard. The pang rang through his brain like a chiming bell. The last thing he heard was the faint dreamlike sound of his father's voice telling Nadine to take him home.

CHAPTER TWENTY

A sudden bright light penetrated Wilmot's crimson eyelids.

'Wilmot! Wilmot, it's time to get up!' said Mum. 'You'll be late for school. I've been calling you for fifteen minutes.'

Wilmot shielded his eyes as his mother pulled open the other curtain, flooding his room with even more winter sunshine. 'Mum?' He touched the back of his aching head, rubbing his fingertips over the tender lump throbbing beneath his raised scalp. 'Where's Dad?'

Mum bit her bottom lip. 'Wilmot, I think you've been...dreaming. Your father is no longer with us, dear.'

'I'm at *home*? I'm in my *bedroom*?'

Mum frowned. 'Where else would you be first thing in the morning?'

'Frank,' he muttered. Wilmot leaped out of bed and lifted his pillow. 'Where is he?'

'Calm down – I've already told you your father isn't here anymore.'

Wilmot scrunched up his duvet and threw it to the floor. 'Where's he gone *now*?'

He moved a stack of books beside his bed to look behind, leaving them to slide across the floor like an opening concertina. Mum stepped back to avoid the rolled-up car posters, which Wilmot was now looking through and discarding like faulty telescopes before lobbing them in her direction.

'Where's Nadine?' asked Wilmot. 'We've got something important to tell you.'

'Nadine just left for school. She told me that she put you to bed last night after,' – she stepped sideways to avoid another flying poster – 'you fell and hit your head on the table. Do you remember falling?' asked Mum.

Wilmot opened his wardrobe without answering his mother. He yanked clothes from the hangers, leaving them to clatter back and forth on the rail, shaking each handful to search for Frank before throwing the clothes to the floor.

'Just how hard did you hit your head?' asked Mum, picking up armfuls of clothes. She watched Wilmot with disbelief as he continued to scour his room.

Wilmot heaved his mattress off the bed and dragged it to the floor, lumping it next to the bedding. 'I can't find him!'

'I know how much you wish your father was still alive, but nothing can bring him back to us. Wilmot, he's been dead for *ten years*. You've just had a *dream*...you're confused.' She sighed deeply as she placed the clothes she was holding on top of his chest of drawers. 'Wilmot, get those things back on the bed. I really don't think you ought to go to school today,' she said, in a more authoritative tone.

'I know he's dead, but...' Wilmot sighed. 'Mum, I saw Dad only hours ago. He *was* real – it was *all* real!' From the bottom upwards, he opened the drawers of his clothes chest and started to rummage through, jamming clothes between the partially shut drawers as he moved from one to the next.

'Wilmot, you've been *dreaming!* And you certainly won't find your father in there! Your father is *dead!*' she persisted.

'*It wasn't a dream!* Dad's created a wonderful place where people who die young can live out their remaining years.' He yanked open the top drawer, leaving it askew, and sifted through. 'Frank, where are you?'

Nothing.

He shoved the stuck drawer several times with his shoulder, but it refused to budge.

'Wilmot, *please* calm down. You're not making any sense. I'm really worried about the knock to your head.'

'I can't find him,' he said. Giving up on the immovable drawer, he slid his fingers through his hair and slumped down on the mattress he'd thrown to the floor. 'You'd believe me if you met Frank.' Burying his head in his hands, he closed his eyes. 'I'm not going *mad*. It can't be a dream. I've been to Dad's world – Madder's World.'

Mum sat down beside Wilmot and stroked his back. 'Dreams can sometimes seem real, even the people you imagine in them, but–'

'But I've been there, and it all feels *too* real to be a dream,' he insisted, looking straight at her with tears welling in his eyes. 'It's an amazing place where you can live out your imaginary thoughts. Remember Dad's idea about storing all your memories in one box – well, he did it! And the boxes can even store what's inside a person's imagination – completely made-up stuff!' He sniffed, trying to hold back the tears as one trickled off his bottom lashes and rolled down his cheek. 'Mum, listen to me, we can go to Madder's World together and visit Dad whenever we want.' He wiped the tear away with the back of his hand.

Mum smiled. 'It sounds wonderful. If only there was such a place. But I think going to yesterday's convention has brought back a lot of memories – it's made your dream seem…' A waft of burnt toast drifted upstairs. She sniffed. 'Stay there…I'll be back in a minute.'

One of the downstairs smoke alarms started bleeping as she rushed out of the room.

Wilmot followed his mother. He leaned over the banister and watched her hurry down the stairs. 'The cellar! I found a cellar in the house!' he shouted.

'You found the cellar! I haven't been down there since your father died. *You* shouldn't have gone down there!' she exclaimed, disappearing from view.

'You know about it? Why didn't you tell me?'

'Your father liked to keep the cellar a secret!' shouted Mum, followed by a bout of coughing. 'I would have told you about it eventually!'

One by one, every smoke alarm in the house joined the deafening chorus.

'So the cellar's real,' he muttered. 'At least I haven't dreamt all of it. I've got to find Nadine.' He leaped down the stairs, coughed his way through the smoke-filled hallway, waving his arms to clear the smoke, and ran out of the front door. 'Nadine!' he shouted, sprinting over the rough road in his socks.

225

Across the road stood Nadine, with her hands on her hips, waiting for him. '*What have you been doing*? I've been waiting for ages – freezing my bum off – out here! You know what she's like – *get to school, Nadine,*' she said, mimicking her mother's voice. 'Have you found him?'

Wilmot hesitated. Staring at Nadine's lips, he went over the last words she'd spoken in his mind. Two conflicting thoughts of elation and trepidation collided in his brain like the impact of a famished eagle's talons gripping the skin of its fleeing prey. Did he want to know the truth? What if it was all nothing more than a vivid dream?

'*Well*...have you found him? Have you found *Frank*?'

'Frank's *real*? Madder's World exists? It's not a dream?'

'Of course it's *real*! You took me there, you idiot! That knock to your head must've done more damage than I'd thought! *Have you got Frank*?'

'No.'

Nadine looked at him wide-eyed. 'You've left Mum in the house with Frank... *alone*?'

'AAAAAH!' came a scream from the house.

'Frank!' cried Wilmot and Nadine.

Taking the lead, Wilmot sprinted across the road, closely followed by Nadine, and ran through the open doorway. A layer of dense smoke hung in the air as he darted through the house following the screams to the kitchen where he found Mum dancing in agony on the trampled, charred remains of the toast.

'Wilmot! Help me! Something's biting my bum!'

'Frank, please, let go!' ordered Wilmot.

Nadine opened the kitchen door as Frank fell with a plop to the floor. The layers of smoke gradually dispersed like early morning mist to reveal the little mucker smiling mischievously up at them from the floor.

The smoke alarm in the kitchen finally stopped bleeping.

'Mum, this is Frank,' said Wilmot.

The remaining smoke alarms bleeped repeatedly in the background.

'*What on earth is that?*' asked Mum.

'I think we've got some explaining to do,' said Nadine, sniggering at the tear in her mother's trousers.

'Look what it did to me!' Mum lifted the flap of torn material.

Wilmot smiled. 'I'm sure you'll forgive him when you hear what we've got to tell you.'

'You might need to sit down first,' said Nadine, offering her mother a stool.

Wilmot laughed. 'I can't wait to tell Dad about *this* the next time we go to Madder's World!'

About the Author

Samantha lives in Norfolk with her husband, four children, two dogs, several chickens and two fish. She plays the piano, enjoys long walks with her dogs, loves cycling and is an avid reader.

It has always been Samantha's ambition to write a children's book. Finally, she took the plunge and wrote Madder's World, combining her writing and the artistic talents of her daughter (Avril) together to bring you this book.

With a head packed full of ideas for a sequel and with two other stories in the pipeline, she hopes this book will be a success, paving the way for all her future projects.

Made in the USA
Charleston, SC
25 November 2013